swamps and how to live off it. You men are going to learn the same.

'You are also going to learn to make friends with the local people, the Malays, who live in the jungle. Many of them used to be head-hunters. It's said that some of them still are. Become their friends. Make sure the heads they take don't include yours.'

JUNGLE WAR

J. ELDRIDGE

A fictional story
based on real-life events

PUFFIN

PUFFIN BOOKS

Published by the Penguin Group
Penguin Books Ltd, 80 Strand, London WC2R 0RL, England
Penguin Group (USA), Inc., 375 Hudson Street, New York, New York 10014, USA
Penguin Books Australia Ltd, 250 Camberwell Road, Camberwell, Victoria 3124, Australia
Penguin Books Canada Ltd, 10 Alcorn Avenue, Toronto, Ontario, Canada M4V 3B2
Penguin Books India (P) Ltd, 11 Community Centre, Panchsheel Park,
New Delhi – 110 017, India
Penguin Group (NZ), cnr Airborne and Rosedale Roads, Albany,
Auckland 1310, New Zealand
Penguin Books (South Africa) (Pty) Ltd, 24 Sturdee Avenue,
Rosebank 2196, South Africa

Penguin Books Ltd, Registered Offices: 80 Strand, London WC2R 0RL, England

www.penguin.com

First published 2004
2

Copyright © Jim Eldridge, 2004

Set in Bookman Old Style by Palimpsest Book Production Ltd, Polmont, Stirlingshire
Made and printed in England by Clays Ltd, St Ives plc

British Library Cataloguing in Publication Data
A CIP catalogue record for this book is available from the British Library

ISBN 0-141-31787-6

To my wife, Lynne

CONTENTS

THE HISTORY OF THE SAS

The SAS developed from the Commandos of the British Army during the Second World War. David Stirling was a lieutenant in the Commandos fighting in the deserts of North Africa in 1941. He believed that a small group of men working covertly behind enemy lines could have a devastating effect on the enemy. His idea was given official approval and so the Special Air Service was born. The newly formed SAS, just 65 men strong, carried out its first operation in November 1941, hitting enemy-held airfields on the North African coast. Throughout 1941 and 1942 it worked with such effectiveness against the German forces in the deserts of North Africa that, in September 1942, the SAS was raised to full regiment status, 1 SAS

Regiment – with a force of 650 men divided into four combat squadrons: A, B, C (the Free French Squadron) and D (the SBS, or Special Boat Section).

In 1943 an additional regiment was formed – 2 SAS – and both regiments fought in the Allied invasion of Italy and Sicily in 1943. Then they took part in the D-Day landings of June 1944, again fighting behind enemy lines.

After the end of the Second World War, the SAS was disbanded. However, many ex-SAS men, who had seen the advantages of such a force, lobbied the War Office for its reinstatement as part of the British Army. The result was that, in 1947, an SAS unit, the Artists Rifles, was formed as part of the Territorial Army. Its official title was 21 SAS (Artists) TA, and many ex-SAS soldiers joined this new outfit. However, the military top brass reduced the SAS in size and importance. Many of the top brass did not like what they considered to be an 'unorthodox organization' within army ranks. By 1949 the SAS consisted of just two squadrons and a signals detachment.

Then, in 1950, came the Malaya conflict.

Malaya had been under British control for many years. In 1948 Britain set up the Federation of Malaya as a step towards independence. However, the minority Chinese population of Malaya, backed by Communist China, resented the domination of the federation by Malay people. Calling themselves the MRLA (the Malayan Races Liberation Army), they began a campaign against the British and Malays in Malaya. During 1950 the MRLA killed 344 civilians and 229 soldiers.

Mike Calvert had fought with Orde Wingate's Chindits behind enemy lines in the Burmese jungle in the Second World War. He had ended the war as Commander of the SAS, and he was given the task of reforming it into a fighting unit to deal with the MRLA. In 1950 Calvert set up a force known as the Malaya Scouts (SAS). This was made up of men from B Company 21 SAS, C Squadron from Rhodesia (now called Zimbabwe) and some reservists. In 1952 the Malaya Scouts became officially known as 22 SAS. 22 SAS fought so successfully behind enemy lines in the jungles of Malaya – living and working with the local peoples – that by 1956 the leaders of the MRLA had fled to Thailand. The Malaya campaign came to an end in 1960, with the SAS having proved itself and its techniques of covert operations.

The strategic structure of an SAS squadron had now been defined. An SAS squadron consists of 64 men in 16 four-man troops. Each four-man troop has to be able to operate independently, living off the local land. As well as being proficient in every kind of weapon and unarmed combat, the troop is capable of dealing with every possible medical emergency.

Further campaigns followed in which the SAS played a key role. In Aden and Borneo (1959–67) and in Oman (1970), SAS soldiers fought behind enemy lines – gaining the support of the local people and militia, blending into the scenery and attacking the enemy where least expected. During the 1970s and 1980s the SAS was a major player in the war against terrorism in Northern Ireland. In 1982 the SAS played an important role in the Falklands

War, and in 1991 and 2003 in the Gulf Wars against Iraq.

Wherever war or terrorism threatens, the SAS is there.

Chapter 1
IN JAIL

I was in an army jail when I first met Major Mike Francis. I was sitting on my bunk, alone in the cell, sentenced to solitary confinement. I heard the key in the lock, then the heavy metal door of the cell swung open. A Military Policeman marched in, swinging a heavy baton in his hand. I could see three more MPs waiting outside the cell.

'Attention, prisoner Taggart!' barked the MP with the baton.

I got up and stood stiffly to attention.

'Someone wants to see you,' he said curtly. 'Quick march!'

I marched out of the cell. Two of the waiting MPs fell into step beside me, the third marched in front, leading the way. The one with the baton brought up the rear.

As we walked along the corridor, the steel tips of our boots ringing on the stone floor, I wondered what lay in store for me. Twice so far I'd been taken out of my cell to a windowless room, where my enemy, Sergeant Andrews, had beaten me with a baton while two of his MP cronies watched, ready to jump in and protect him if I fought back. Sergeant Andrews had called it 'teaching me a lesson'. Beating me was against regulations, and after the first time I'd complained to a senior officer. Andrews simply said that he'd hit me only in self-defence because I had attacked him first. It was a lie, but who were the officers going to believe: a sergeant or me, an ordinary private in a military jail for a list of offences?

So the second time Andrews beat me – which was to pay me back for 'squealing on him', as he put it – I'd taken the blows and just glared back at him, biting my lip to stop from yelling out, determined not to let him have the pleasure of hearing me cry out in pain. And I knew that if I fought back, he and his cronies would beat me senseless with their

7

batons. Then they'd claim they'd only been defending themselves against my attack. Well, I decided that if Andrews and his pals started beating me again today, I would defend myself and bring down as many of them with me as I could. Sergeant Andrews would be the first I'd go for. He was a sadistic bully, and I was going to pay him back for what he'd done to me. I didn't care what happened to me after that.

We marched down another stone corridor and stopped outside a door. The MP at the front opened it and barked, 'Inside, prisoner Taggart!'

I took a deep breath and stepped into the room. I clenched and unclenched my fists, getting myself prepared mentally for what I thought lay ahead, ready to dodge the first baton swing and go into the attack. But, to my surprise, Sergeant Andrews wasn't in the room. Instead, a smallish man in army uniform, with lots of brass on his shoulder, was pacing around the windowless room. A table and two chairs were the only furniture. A thin paper file lay on the table. I spotted that it had my name on it: Private Ian Taggart.

'Prisoner Taggart, sir!' the leading MP announced in a loud crisp voice.

The man nodded and said, 'Leave him here. I'll call when I need you.'

The MPs looked taken aback at this and exchanged swift, awkward glances. Then the leading one began, 'With respect, sir, the prisoner is violent –'

But the small man cut him off sharply and snapped, 'Are you questioning an order?'

The MP gulped before replying, 'No, sir.'

'Then I repeat, I'll call you when I need you.'

There was a brief moment's hesitation before the leading MP gave a smart salute, swung about turn and marched out of the room with the others. All the time I had been standing stiffly to attention, wondering what the hell was going on.

The small man went to the door, shut it and gestured to one of the chairs.

'At ease, Taggart,' he said. 'Sit down.'

Still baffled by what was happening, I went and sat down. The small man took the chair opposite me at the table. If he was worried about the fact that he was alone in a room with someone described as 'violent', he didn't seem to show it. I learned later why: if I'd tried anything he could have killed me with just one blow. He had reflexes like a cat and, despite his small size, he looked as strong as anyone I've ever met.

'My name's Francis,' he introduced himself. 'Major Mike Francis. For the moment, you can call me Major.' He opened a packet of cigarettes and offered them to me. 'Smoke?'

I shook my head. 'No thank you, Major, I don't smoke.'

'Wise man,' nodded the Major. However, he took one of the cigarettes himself, popped it into his mouth and lit it with a big metal American cigarette-lighter.

'So,' he said, 'I hear you've got a string of charges against you. Absent without leave. Theft of a military vehicle. Striking a superior officer.'

'Yes, sir,' I answered stiffly.

'How old are you, Taggart?'

It was a pointless question. If the Major had my file on the table, he already knew the answer. But I was used to pointless questions in the army. I played along with it, as I always had done, ever since I joined up.

'I'm nineteen, sir,' I replied.

The Major nodded and said, 'If you are found guilty of the charges against you at your court martial, you face a long time in jail. You'll be an old man by the time you get out. Well, old in your terms, that is.'

I kept my expression blank, not wanting to reveal my emotions to this man. I didn't know what this was all about, but my experience of the army so far had shown that it paid to be suspicious of everyone and everything.

'I did the crimes, sir; I'll take my punishment,' I said.

'So you admit they were crimes,' said the Major casually. 'Interesting.'

I didn't reply. Never offer an answer unless you're asked a direct question – that was another lesson I'd learned.

The Major asked a direct question. 'Tell me about these crimes of yours. What happened?'

I hesitated, wary, before I answered simply, 'It's all in the reports, sir.'

'I know,' said the Major. 'I've read them. I want to hear *your* version.'

What the hell, I thought. Why not. In for a penny, in for a pound. I'll tell him the truth. If he doesn't like it, they can only throw me back in the cell again. Back to Sergeant Andrews. I had nothing to lose.

'I got a letter from my Aunt Celia to say my father was in hospital in York, dying. I asked for compassionate leave to see him before he died. It was refused.'

'By Sergeant Andrews?'

I was surprised at the Major introducing Andrews's name into the conversation. I wondered whether it was some sort of trap for me set by Andrews, but, then again, I thought: what if it is. I'm being asked for the truth, so I'll tell it.

'Yes, sir,' I said.

'Continue,' said the Major.

I carried on with my story.

'There was no way I wasn't going to see my father before he died. So I took a vehicle and drove to York. I saw my father in the hospital and sat with him while he died. Afterwards I came back here.'

'Which is where you assaulted a superior officer,' said the Major.

'Sergeant Andrews was unhappy that I'd gone to see my father in defiance of his orders,' I said. 'He told me what I'd done had made him look a fool, and he wasn't going to let me get away with it. He got two of his pals to hold me, and he beat me up. When his pals let go of me I hit him. Just once.'

'And knocked him unconscious?' queried the Major.

'It was a lucky punch,' I admitted.

I didn't add that I felt great seeing Andrews crumple to the ground, but that I'd been paying for it with beatings from him ever since.

Major Francis nodded thoughtfully, as if he was thinking over what I'd just told him. Next he said in a calm voice, 'I'm going to give you the chance to get out of here.'

I was surprised at this. I looked at the Major warily.

'And do what?' I asked suspiciously.

'Work for me,' said the Major. 'I'm setting

13

up a new squadron for my regiment, the Special Air Service. We're fighting a war against terrorists in Malaya. I need men.'

'Why me?' I asked. 'I'm in jail. The army says I'm a criminal.'

'Not yet they don't,' said the Major. 'You haven't been court-martialled. I think I can deal with your charges, if you agree to join us.'

'But why me?' I insisted again. 'Especially when it's obvious the regular army and I don't see eye to eye.'

Major Francis began to make his points, ticking off each on a separate finger as he did so.

'One, you showed loyalty to your father, and you used your initiative to get to see him at all costs. You achieved your objective. Two, you came back. That shows integrity and courage. Three, you took a bad beating and yet you knocked out your attacker with one punch. That shows endurance and physical courage. Loyalty, initiative, integrity, physical strength, courage. An ability to think on your own and put your plan into action. Those are the qualities in men I'm looking for.

14

'Now, you have a choice. You can rot in this stinking jail, or you can come out to Malaya and be in extreme danger in a stinking jungle. Which is it to be?'

And that's how I joined the SAS.

Chapter 2
A BUNCH OF CRIMINALS

Two days later I was on my way overseas. All charges against me had been dropped. On the day I left the jail, Sergeant Andrews came to see me in my cell. As always, he was backed up by three of his mates from the Military Police.

'I don't know what strings you pulled to get out of here, Taggart,' he snarled, 'but I'm letting you know that this isn't over. One way or another, I'm going to get you.'

'If you're thinking of trying to provoke me into a fight so you can keep me behind bars, think again,' I snapped back. 'I agree this isn't over between us. The next time I see you when I'm outside, you'd better make sure you're armed, or you've got lots of friends round you, because I'm going to get you for what you did to me.'

Andrews glared at me, the long heavy baton twitching in his hand. For a moment I thought he was going to attack me again. But he didn't.

'You're scum, Taggart,' he said. 'People like you can't take discipline. There's no room for rubbish like you in this army.'

With that, he left, his MP pals following him.

After I left the jail, I reported to my barracks and packed up my kit. The place was empty; the rest of my squad were out on patrol, so there was no one for me to say goodbye to.

I carried my kitbag over to the Duty Office and signed myself out. Everyone in the camp knew I was leaving for 'special duty' overseas, but no one seemed to know exactly what those duties were. I didn't give any explanations. I simply said, 'Private Taggart 85867936 reporting for transfer.'

I was passed a load of forms to sign before being sent to wait at the transport bay. After about an hour, a battered looking single-decker army bus pulled up. The driver got out and said, 'Taggart?'

I nodded and got on the bus. Nearly all the other seats were taken; there were just a few empty ones near the front. I sat down next to a soldier in a double seat just behind the driver.

The driver engaged the clutch and the bus moved off, the engine jolting and coughing and spluttering.

'Is this the best they could find?' I asked.

'If it's luxury you want, don't join the SAS,' grunted the soldier next to me.

'Who said anything about luxury,' I responded. 'A bus that won't break down would be good.'

The soldier nodded and said, 'My name's Benny Watts.'

'Ian Taggart,' I replied.

'You volunteered for this lot as well, then?' Benny asked.

I nodded.

Benny grinned. He was short and stocky, with a cheerful look about him, and his dark hair cut very short, army style.

'Heading off to a stinking jungle and certain death!' he chuckled. 'You must have been in a lot of trouble in your own unit, boy.'

'Not at all,' I said defensively. 'It just seemed a good idea – to actually get out there and fight an enemy instead of doing useless things, like painting coal black whenever some VIP visits our base.'

'True,' nodded Benny. 'I was going to be court-martialled for striking a senior officer, a lieutenant.' He shrugged. 'I had to do it because he was about to fire a heavy-artillery gun that would have killed all of my unit. He wouldn't listen to me when I said it was blocked and it would backfire. He insisted we all stood to attention while he fired the thing. There was only one way to stop him and that was to knock him out. So I did.

'Afterwards they found out I was dead right. The barrel of the gun *was* blocked and we'd all have been blown to smithereens if it had gone off. But I still got charged for striking a senior officer.'

'I hit a sergeant,' I admitted.

'Did you knock him out with one punch?' Benny challenged.

I nodded.

'OK,' said Benny with grudging reluctance. 'We're equal there. But I knocked out a lieutenant, so that's one better than a sergeant.'

The soldier behind us leaned forward and said proudly, 'I hit a major!'

'Did you knock him out?' Benny asked him.

'No,' said the soldier.

'Then it doesn't count,' said Benny.

'Course it does,' said the soldier. 'You can get shot for hitting a major.'

'Rubbish,' said Benny.

'I'm still ahead of both of you, with hitting a major,' insisted the soldier.

'Oh yeah?' said Benny. 'We'll see about that.'

Benny stood up, turned and addressed the rest of the bus, calling out, 'Anyone hit someone higher than the rank of major?'

A hand at the back went up.

'I punched a colonel,' said this soldier, a huge man with close-cropped red hair.

'Did you knock him out?' demanded Benny.

The soldier nodded. 'Of course.'

'OK,' said Benny. 'You win.'

And with that he sat down.

I looked out of the window. I couldn't

help but think: I'm sitting with a bus-load of criminals. Just what sort of unit have I joined?

Chapter 3
THE JUNGLE

When our bus pulled into Northolt aerodrome, I saw that there were already two other buses parked up, with about seventy men standing around, their kitbags beside them. With the men getting off our bus and joining them, that made us a hundred strong.

'We're the Renegades' Regiment,' joked Benny, looking at the assembled men.

We certainly looked a motley bunch, all of us from different regiments. And, from the stories we'd swapped on the bus, all with different histories but one thing in common: difficulties with our regular regiments.

A huge RAF transport plane was on the runway about half a mile away.

'You ever been in a plane before?' asked Benny.

I shook my head.

'You?' I asked.

'No,' said Benny. 'I like to keep my feet on the ground. Still, there's a first time for everything.'

The sound of a vehicle approaching made me look round. The vehicle pulled up and Major Francis jumped out.

'Right, men,' he said, 'glad you could all make it. Let's get moving. Next stop: Singapore.'

In fact our next stop wasn't Singapore, but Germany. However, not for long: just enough time to refuel, go to the toilet, and then we were off again. After that we had about four more stops to refuel the plane, get food and water for us, and to stretch our legs. I remember we stopped in Iran and India, but after that it all became a bit of a blur.

On the flight we talked and got to know one another. I learned that we weren't all criminals or refugees from jail. One of the older men, Eddie Kershaw, was in his thirties and had been with Wingate's Chindits, a group of British commandos. They had fought behind Japanese lines in the jungles of Burma during the Second World War, and won.

'I first came out to South-east Asia and into the jungle in nineteen forty-three,' Eddie told me and Benny. 'I was eighteen then, fifteen years ago.'

'What was it like?' asked Benny.

'It was the best time of my life,' replied Eddie. 'But at the same time, the most frightening. Hot, stinking, treacherous jungle: a mixture of swamp and tree roots crawling with insects and disease. We never knew when the Japanese might find us. And we were heavily outnumbered. That first time, in nineteen forty-three, three thousand of us went into the jungle against eighty thousand Japanese, and only two thousand of us came out. I went back in again with the next lot in nineteen forty-four. This time there were twenty-three thousand of us. Much better odds. The Americans went into Burma as well that second time, from the north. Merrill's Marauders, they were called. Wingate himself died when his plane crashed in the jungle just before we started that second campaign.'

'What was he like?' I asked. 'Orde Wingate.'

'He was great,' replied Eddie. 'He had a big beard and long arms. And he was one of the untidiest men you ever saw. Someone once said he looked like he put his clothes on with a shovel! He looked a bit like someone had put clothes on a gorilla. But he was clever. And tough. And he'd never ask anyone to do what he couldn't do himself.' Eddie nodded towards the front of the plane, where the Major was sitting. 'Just like the Major there. He was the same.'

Benny looked at the Major, interest on his face.

'You mean he was in the Chindits as well?' he whispered.

Eddie nodded.

'Oh yes,' he said. 'I was with him during both campaigns. Tough as they come. He got shot through the arm during the second campaign. Broke it in two places. He got us to tie it up for him, and then carried on with one arm. You should see him load and fire a gun with one hand. He took out a Japanese machine-gun post all on his own, just with the one arm. That's why, when he came and saw me at my unit and asked me if I'd like to join up for this caper, I jumped at the chance. He's a fair man, and, if he's with you, you've got a chance of surviving.'

Afterwards, when Benny and I were on our own, Benny jerked his head in Eddie's direction and said, 'If we get split up into different units, I'm going to try and get in the same lot as Eddie there. A man who's been in the jungle before will know what he's doing.'

After an air journey that seemed to last for days, we finally arrived in Singapore. The first thing I noticed as I stepped out of the plane was the heat. The air was damp, wet and hot. I sweated just with the exertion of breathing in and out.

Eddie saw me wiping the sweat from my forehead, and he came up to me and grinned.

'This is nothing, son,' he said. 'This is *cool* compared to the jungle. Just you wait and see.'

We were taken by bus to the Army HQ, which looked much the same as an army base back home in England, except for the enormously tall palm trees round it.

Our barracks – like all the rest of the buildings on the base – were wooden huts with roofs made of palm leaves.

'Loads of palm trees everywhere,' commented Benny. 'I wonder if that means loads of coconuts? I love coconuts. I won one at a fair once and it tasted fantastic.'

The hundred of us checked in, bagged our bunks and grabbed a meal in the mess (the canteen). Then we assembled on a patch of green near the parade ground to be addressed by Major Francis. By now it was late afternoon. The flies and insects buzzed around us. Along with the other men, I swatted at them with my hand.

'Don't worry about the insects,' the Major told us. 'When you've been in the jungle for a while you'll have got used to them. They'll still be eating you alive, but you'll have got used to them.'

He paced around for a moment, as if he was gathering his thoughts, before he said, 'You men are D Squadron, Special Air Service. The SAS is an unorthodox unit in the British Army. We don't work by the same rules as the rest. As you will have realized, the men of the SAS are volunteers.

At any point you can resign and go back to your units.'

'Or back to a cell,' whispered Benny beside me.

'You men have volunteered to go into the jungle and fight the enemy,' continued the Major. 'Therefore, you need to know who and what your enemy is, and just what kind of fight this is going to be.

'It's going to be a dirty fight. That's because our enemy fights dirty. We're not going to beat them by using traditional army methods. We have to be as cunning and as devious as they are.

'Our enemy lives in the jungle. It's their home, so they know all the dangers, all the swamps and how to live off the jungle. You men are going to learn the same.

'You are also going to learn to make friends with the local people, the Malays, who live in the jungle. Many of them used to be head-hunters. It's said that some of them still are. Become their friends. Make sure the heads they take don't include yours.'

At the mention of 'head-hunters', Benny and I exchanged concerned looks. Fighting terrorists was one thing. Coming up against people who collected heads was altogether another thing.

The Major was continuing with his pep talk. 'The people we are fighting are not the Malays. Our enemies are Chinese Communists who fought in Malaya against the Japanese during the Second World War. We gave them the weapons to use against the Japanese. It was a good way of protecting Malaya from the Japanese. When the Japanese surrendered and left Malaya, the Chinese stayed. They now want Malaya for their own, as a Communist republic, independent of Britain. If that happens, the truth is it won't be independent. It will still be a colony, but this time a colony of Communist China.

'To try to force the British to leave Malaya, these Communist terrorists have been carrying out sneaky guerrilla attacks on rubber plantations, on police stations, as well as on ordinary people. Their campaign of terror has been going on for ten years, since nineteen forty-eight. So far they have killed over a thousand British civilians, and about the same number of police officers. They use everything at their disposal. Not just guns, but machetes and knives, even bows and arrows.'

'I wonder if they collect heads as well?' Benny muttered beside me.

'The Major will collect yours if you don't shut up and listen,' whispered Eddie sharply.

The Major had fallen silent while this little bit of whispering went on, and he paced around a bit more. Again, he made it appear as if he was gathering his thoughts before he spoke, but my guess was he had heard Benny whispering and was letting him know that he'd better follow Eddie's advice and shut up while the Major was talking. Benny did shut up. The Major continued his briefing.

'For these past ten years the regular British Army has been fighting the terrorists and has been slowly winning the battle against them. There is now just a hard core of these terrorists left – we calculate about a hundred of them – but they are the most dangerous. Their leader is a man called Chung Lo. The last photograph taken of him was over ten years ago, so, to be honest, that picture won't be much use to you. He's short, but so are many of his comrades.

'Chung Lo and his followers have taken refuge in the Telok Anson swamp – an area eighteen miles by ten miles. It's a place impossible for the regular army to fight in because of the difficulty of the terrain. It's one hundred and eighty square miles of stinking swamps mixed with fast-running rivers and thick jungle – many of the trees are two hundred feet high. There's very little daylight. A lot of the plants have thorns on them which will rip skin to pieces.

'You can't wear too much protective clothing in the jungle because of the high temperature – it's about eighty degrees Fahrenheit. The humidity level – the amount of water in the air – is so high that it will rot your clothes as you walk.

'Much of the time you will be wading through swamp water up to chest height. Leeches will crawl through any gap in your clothing, stick to your body and suck your blood. They'll get everywhere. They'll fall off you when they've had enough blood from you; even so it's not a pleasant experience. Don't try and pull them off. If you do, their jaws – which they will have used to bite into you – will remain stuck in

31

your skin and the wound may become infected. I'm afraid there are only two ways to remove leeches – with heat or with salt.

'As you can see, the terrorists have chosen their hiding place carefully. It's filled with natural defences.

'It's impossible just to drop bombs into the jungle and hope we'll hit the enemy. If we did so, the chances are we'd kill hundreds of Malays as well. We have to keep them on our side at all costs.

'Our enemy is completely ruthless. The Communists have inflicted a reign of terror on the local people. If they think that the locals have helped us in any way, they kill some of them in retaliation.

'Getting to the Telok Anson swamp isn't easy. Going across country would take days, if not weeks. That would give the Communists time to prepare. We need to hit them as quickly as possible, catch them by surprise. So, we'll be dropped by parachute as close to the swamp as we can get. Those of you who've never parachuted out of a plane before will be trained.'

Parachutes! I must admit I had mixed feelings about this when I heard the Major say it. On the one hand, I really wanted to feel what it would be like floating through the air. But, on the other hand, what if my chute didn't open?

'The plan is that we will go into the swamp in ten units of ten men,' said the Major. 'Each unit will start from the edge of the swamp at a different point and head in towards the middle, where we believe the Communists' HQ is. Think of it like ten spokes on a wheel, all aiming for the centre. We're giving the terrorists no chance to escape. Whichever way they try to leave the swamp, they will come up against one of our units. Keep in radio contact with each other. Report any sightings to the other units.'

The Major smiled.

'For those of you who think we officers will be living a life of luxury while you men are suffering in the swamp, I'd better let you know that I will be with you in the jungle, leading one of the units myself.

'Now, you know what your task will be. As I said before, the SAS is a force of volunteers. If any man wishes to withdraw and return to his unit, come and see me afterwards. There's no room in the SAS for passengers or for people who aren't one hundred and ten per cent committed.'

With that we were dismissed. Most of us stayed around, watching to see if anyone approached Major Francis to talk about quitting. Interestingly, no one did. Either what faced us back in the regular army was too awful to return to, or the thought of going into the jungle and fighting a real enemy was too exciting a prospect to miss. Or maybe it was just that we'd spent two days stuck on the most boring plane journey imaginable, and no one could bear the thought of getting back on the plane and repeating it. Whatever the reason, we all stayed.

Chapter 4
TRAINING

We spent the next four weeks in training. And not the sort of training we did back home in England, which usually consisted of marching and exercises like running and jumping over vaulting horses. This training was teaching us about how to survive in the jungle.

We learned that our most useful tool was the *parang*, a kind of machete. The only way to get through thick vegetation was to hack at it with a *parang* to clear a path. But when clearing bamboo, you had to be careful not to leave spikes of it sticking up, because if anyone stumbled and fell on one of them, it would be like a spear going right through their body.

We learned about the different sorts of plants we'd find. That the atap and rattan plants had thorns at the end of their leaves that were as sharp and as vicious as fish hooks. If you got caught on one, you had to back off and untangle yourself from it slowly, or it would tear a chunk of your flesh out.

We learned which plants we could eat for food, like the berries of the bignay bush, or the fruit of the sweetsop tree. Some fruits and berries could be eaten raw, while others had to be cooked, like the yam bean, for example. Its root could be dug up and eaten. I tried it. It had a sweet nutty taste – strange, but OK. The seeds of the plant, however, would make you ill if you ate them raw. Water spinach grew in the swamps and the young leaves could be boiled and eaten. The bamboo tree was a great source of food: the young shoots growing at the base of the tree and the seeds could be eaten.

We were also warned about plants that looked very similar to all the edible ones, but which were poisonous. These plants may have looked very safe, but they could kill you if you ate them by mistake. One such plant was the white mangrove – small, with deadly round, white berries. The sap caused blisters on the skin and could blind you. Then there was the pangi tree, every part of which was poisonous. There was another plant whose fruit looked just like a strawberry, except that it was lethal if eaten.

We learned how to make camp, including building a bamboo frame to raise your bed off the ground so the insects didn't crawl all over you and eat you alive.

We learned how to hunt: how to trap an animal; how to fish without using a rod; how to start a fire without using matches or a lighter.

First aid, too, wasn't the sort we had back home in England. As well as teaching us about bandages, we learned how to sew up our own wounds, and how to use jungle plants as medicines. Some plants could be used as antidotes to snake-bites from the likes of the Malay viper or the krait, whose venom was twice as poisonous as a cobra's.

Weapons training also came into it, of course. We were allowed to choose our own weapons from the armoury. I noticed that Eddie chose an American M1 carbine rifle.

'Why that one?' I asked him. 'Why not

a Sten gun? Something with a bit of power.'

Eddie passed me the short-barrelled rifle.

'Hold it,' he said.

I took it, running my hands over its wooden stock and the short barrel.

'It's light,' I said.

'Exactly,' said Eddie.

'But it doesn't have much range,' I said, pointing at the short barrel.

'We're going into the jungle,' said Eddie. 'How far do you think you'll be able to see when you're surrounded on all sides by trees? Another thing, the M1 is the most reliable weapon I've used. It doesn't jam like some of the others.'

Right, I thought, if the M1 is good enough for Eddie, it's good enough for me.

Because we were going to be dropped in by air, that meant training for those who'd never parachuted. This consisted of climbing up a tall platform and jumping off it on a rope. At the last moment, you released the rope, hit the ground and rolled forwards. We also learned the theory of what to do if the strings of our chute got tangled up when it opened. If the strings got tangled, the chute couldn't open properly and you'd just fall like a stone. If that happened to any of us, we were to turn round slowly in the air until the strings untangled. Hopefully, by then we were still high enough off the ground to make a reasonably slow descent.

'When are we going to go up in a plane and do a real parachute drop?' complained Chester Harris one night, after yet another session of jumping from the high platform. Chester was from Newcastle and very impatient.

'When we go into action,' said Eddie.

'Why not before?' asked Chester.

'In case you get it wrong and die,' said Eddie. 'If you die in training, that means one less man on the troop when we go into action.'

I must admit, it didn't sound encouraging.

We also learned some basic words in Malay, as well as some simple Chinese, like the words for 'Hands up' and 'Stop or I shoot'. I noticed we weren't told the Chinese for 'I surrender'.

At the end of the four weeks, after the hardest training I'd ever done in my entire life, the squadron was split into the ten units. I was pleased that Benny and I were in the same one. I'd got quite attached to his cheery manner. If we were going to be stuck in this nightmare of a jungle, it would be helpful to be with someone who had a good sense of humour. We were both pleased that Eddie Kershaw was also with us. It was great to think we were going to be with someone who had first-hand experience of jungle warfare.

The best news for me came when we heard that Major Francis was going to be commanding our unit, Unit One, in the operation. From what Eddie had said about him, it seemed to me and Benny that having the Major with us gave us that much more of a chance to survive.

The night before we were due to make our parachute drop into the swamp, Major Francis assembled the whole squadron for a last pep talk.

'Right, men,' he said, 'you've been practising living and fighting in the jungle. Tomorrow comes the real thing. I won't lie to you: it's going to be much harder than anything you've done this last month in training. For one thing, the enemy will be trying their very best to kill you. And, at the end of the day, there'll be no going back to a bunk in your barracks. The jungle will be your bed, it will be your kitchen, it will be your hospital and, if you lose concentration, it will be your grave.

'We can win this fight. We've beaten a jungle enemy before; we can do it again. But we have to work together. Look after one another. And remember, "He who dares, wins". So, get a good night's sleep, men. We set off for the Telok Anson swamp at first light.'

Chapter 5
INTO THE SWAMP

At dawn the next morning we clambered into the Beverley transport plane, our chutes strapped to our backs and our rucksacks and rifles strapped round our bodies.

We were going up in two planes: fifty men in each one. We were to be dropped by unit, at intervals of four miles, round the perimeter of Telok Anson swamp. Although jumping by day meant that there was a chance our chutes would be seen, you can't drop into jungle at night, not with all those trees. You couldn't see where you'd be going and might easily be skewered on one of the branches.

In my unit there were Major Francis, Benny, Eddie, Chester and five other blokes: Tony Gerson from Cornwall; Bill Stevens from Yorkshire, who'd been in the Medical Corps before joining the SAS; Jack Roberts from Belfast in Northern Ireland; Pete Shaw from Bristol; and 'Mack' Mackenzie from Glasgow. Me and Benny were both Londoners, and Eddie was originally from Birmingham.

The mood inside the Beverley was jokey at first after we took off, but it settled down into an awkward silence. I don't think any of us were looking forward to parachuting into the jungle. During our training we'd heard stories of what had happened to men who landed in a bamboo tree . . . If you were lucky, you just got caught on a branch and ended up hanging a hundred feet up in the air. You hoped you could swing into the tree and climb down the rope we'd all been issued with. It was two hundred feet long, with knots every eighteen inches for handholds.

I was told that earlier groups had been issued with lengths of webbing. They could fix it to a branch and abseil down at speed, the webbing going through a metal D-ring on their uniform. The problem was that the webbing had bumps where the separate lengths were stitched together. Some men had abseiled down fast, hit a bump in the webbing and stopped so suddenly that the force of it had broken their arms.

I looked out of the window at the ground below. Thick jungle. Mile after mile of trees. Every so often there was a clearing. Some of them looked so small that I knew there was every chance of hitting a tree when you landed in them.

Finally, we came to the jungle that hid the Telok Anson swamp. From the air it looked so dense that it seemed impossible for people to actually live in it.

The Beverley began to circle.

'OK, Unit One, line up and get ready to jump!' called one of the plane's crew as he moved to the open doorway.

Major Francis was first up. He walked over to the doorway, using one of the metal crossbars inside the cabin as a handhold. Benny Watts joined him as second in line. I stepped in to be third man out. One by one the rest of Unit One lined up behind me.

The plane circled over a clearing at the edge of the jungle of tall trees.

'OK,' said the crewman, and he tapped the Major on the shoulder.

'See you chaps down on the ground,' said the Major, and he leaped out of the doorway.

The crewman tapped Benny on the shoulder, and Benny jumped. I felt the crewman tap me on my shoulder, and I also threw myself forwards out of the plane.

I fell, plunging down like a stone, my arms and legs wide like a giant X-shape to keep myself stable. I remembered my instructions. Stay level. Don't let yourself go upside down or you can get tangled up in your chute when it opens. Don't let yourself fall head over heels or, again, you'll get tangled up. Use your arms and legs to keep you level as you fall. As I fell I counted down . . . one elephant . . . two elephants . . . three elephants . . . then I pulled my rip-cord.

For a second, as my canopy opened and caught the thermals coming up from the jungle, I shot back up into the air. Soon I started to drop. It was an amazing feeling, drifting down in space. It felt like

I was just hanging there, but then I saw the tops of the trees rushing up towards me.

I pulled at the cords of the chute to steer away from the trees, because the wind was pushing me straight at them. Down, down, down I came, every second getting nearer and nearer to the trees . . . And then my chute got caught on a branch and I was swinging right into a tree. I put up my arms to ward off branches hitting me in the face, like a boxer fending off blows from his opponent. I thumped against a branch and swung back.

I was dangling about thirty feet off the ground. I pulled out the coil of rope and tied one end to the strongest branch near me. Then I began to climb down. I made it to the ground and found Major Francis and Benny already there.

Above us, the rest of our unit were floating down on their chutes. Within a few minutes they were on the ground. We ditched our chutes and sorted out our supplies and weapons. Laden with our rucksacks and ammunition, and with rifles at the ready, we followed Major

Francis into the jungle, into the Telok Anson swamp. We were going into the enemy's stronghold.

Chapter 6
THE TRAP

As part of our training we'd spent time in the jungle in Singapore, to get us used to the kind of terrain we were going into. The Singapore jungle had been hot and damp, a tangle of tree roots and swamp and bog, with very little light coming down through the trees. Those conditions had been bad enough; the Telok Anson swamp was worse. The trees were higher and closer together. It was darker. And wetter. And hotter. Maybe it was made worse because I knew that the enemy were there, waiting for us.

'Watch out for scorpions,' Eddie whispered to me as we pushed our way slowly through the tangle of vegetation.

'I thought scorpions lived in hot sandy places,' I said. 'Desert, places like that.'

'They also live here,' said Eddie. 'Them,

and ants, and hornets, and loads of other creepy-crawlies.'

Major Francis was taking point, which meant he went first. He moved slowly, checking the ground in front of him, stopping every now and then to listen and look up at the trees before continuing.

As we moved through the jungle, going slowly, I became aware of the sounds. The chatter of monkeys, a peculiar high-pitched noise. And birds, squawking and chirping, their wings fluttering as they flew from branch to branch in the canopy high above us. The drip drip drip of water dropping from the tops of the trees and working its way down, from leaf to leaf. Sounds of slithering in the undergrowth: snakes.

'Don't worry too much about the snakes,' Eddie whispered. 'They'll do their best to keep out of your way. They don't like us any more than we like them. But don't tread on one, or it'll take your leg off.'

'In one bite?' I asked Eddie, in awe.

'If it's a crusher, it'll crush your leg. If it's a biter, it'll sink enough poison into you that your leg will have to be taken off. Either way, you'll lose a leg. So watch where you put your feet.'

The overriding sound was that of insects, crunching and chomping their way through the vegetation. It was like hearing a constant whispering noise all around you.

It took us an hour to travel about half a mile.

'At this rate we'll all be old men before we finally come face to face with the Communists,' complained Chester.

'The Major knows what he's doing,' said Eddie. 'Trust me, you don't know what dangers are here.'

'Don't talk to me about danger!' Chester spat back. 'I come from Newcastle. There's danger on every street corner up there. I'll tell you the proper way to do this and that's the way you deal with any bully. You go straight in and belt him one. All this hanging about, peering around every bush before we make a move, it just lets the terrorists know we're scared of them.'

'No,' replied Eddie, shaking his head. 'It lets them know we're not stupid. Don't forget, these Chinese Communists know this jungle. They've been hiding out in it for years. It's theirs.'

'Not any more,' snapped Chester harshly. 'I'm in it now. It's mine.'

We'd all been scouring the undergrowth for tracks. Now Jack Roberts called out, 'The plants are trodden down over here! It looks like someone's walked this way to the edge of the swamp.'

'*Careful*,' warned Eddie. 'It may be booby-trapped.'

'What with?' asked Jack.

'Anything,' put in Major Francis. 'Hand-grenades left propped against a piece of wood with the pins partway out. As soon as you kick the wood, the pins fall out and . . . bang! You've lost a leg. If you're lucky, that is. Or mantraps.'

'They don't scare me,' scowled Chester. 'I'll soon see if there are any traps or not.'

With that, Chester moved forwards along the trodden-down plants, eyes down on the ground in front of him, poking about with the barrel of his rifle.

'Go slowly!' snapped the Major.

If Chester heard, he didn't pay much attention. He ploughed on, regardless.

'We'd better follow him in case he blows himself up accidentally,' said Tony Gerson. 'Someone had better be around to pick up the pieces.'

'I'll do it,' muttered Eddie. 'In fact, I'll head him off. If he does set anything off, it'll just let the enemy know we're here.'

Eddie pushed past me and Tony, heading after Chester. The rest of us hurried after Eddie and caught up with him as he neared the edge of the swamp. Chester was already standing on the marshes at the edge of the thick brown waters of the swamp.

'They went this way,' he said, pointing across the swamp to the bank at the far side. 'You can see by that broken branch over there – that's where they landed.'

'Maybe,' said Eddie.

'There's no "maybe" about it,' snorted Chester. 'Well, I'm going after them.'

And he moved towards the swamp.

Eddie suddenly leaped forward, reaching out to grab him and shouting 'No!', but he was too late. Chester jumped straight into the sludgy water, right up to his shoulders, and as he went in he screamed. It was a terrifying sound, the pain of it tore through all of us.

Tony and me who were nearest to the swamp went to jump in to pull Chester out, but Eddie stopped us.

'*No!*' he snapped firmly.

I watched in horror as Chester thrashed about in the water before he slumped and his head went under the dark water.

Major Francis had joined us by this time. His face looked grim. He and Eddie sat on the edge of the swamp, their feet in the water, and then they slipped in. When their feet touched the bottom they moved slowly towards where Chester's head was now floating on the surface, all the time moving their arms in front of them, as if feeling their way through the water.

Major Francis obviously found something, because he gave a questioning look at Eddie, who nodded grimly. Both men ducked underwater. About twenty seconds later Chester's body began to rise out of the water, and we saw that the Major and Eddie were beneath him, lifting Chester up, lifting him clear of something.

Eddie moved back towards the swamp's

edge, carrying Chester with him. Tony, Benny and I gathered round to help to drag Chester out.

Chester was still breathing, but his eyes were shut. His clothes were a sodden mess. I assumed they were wet from the swamp, until I noticed the liquid seeping from his thighs and round his waist. He was bleeding.

I looked towards the swamp and saw the Major pulling himself out of it. In his hand he carried two bamboo stakes, sharpened at one end.

'The track of trodden plants was a trap,' he said. 'Bamboo stakes just below the surface, stuck in the mud.' The Major threw the stakes down on the ground in disgust. 'Shaw, Stevens,' he said, 'you're best at first aid. See what you can do for him.'

Pete Shaw and Bill Stevens set to work, cutting away Chester's clothes round the wounds where the bamboo stakes had gone into him.

'Gerson,' the Major said to Tony. 'Get on the radio. Tell HQ we've got a man badly injured. Bamboo stakes through the legs and belly. We'll need a chopper with medics to get him to hospital. Give them the map reference for where we came in so they know where to set down.'

While Tony cranked up the radio, the Major turned to the rest of us.

'Luckily for Harris we're not far into the jungle, so we can still get him out. If we'd been a few days further in, we'd have had to do what we could for him ourselves. Still, I need two volunteers to carry Harris out and wait with him until the chopper arrives.'

Bill Stevens put up his hand.

'I'll go, Major,' he said. 'I'm ex-Medical Corps. Chester's going to need help to stay alive before the chopper gets here.'

'I'll go as well,' nodded Pete Shaw.

'Good lads,' said the Major. 'Once you've put him on the chopper, come after us. We'll leave markers to show you our route.'

Tony had been speaking into the radio while this had been going on. He turned to the Major.

'HQ says they'll have a chopper at the edge of the jungle as soon as they can, sir.'

'Good,' nodded the Major. Turning back

to us, he said, 'I hate to use what's happened as a lesson, but take it as one. Expect traps everywhere. The Communists aren't here to play games. Every one of you must be careful. We can't afford to lose any more men.'

Chapter 7

HEAD-HUNTERS

With Bill Stevens and Pete Shaw carrying Chester out of the jungle on a makeshift stretcher, our unit was reduced to seven. We moved forward until the jungle ended and we were face to face with the slimy water of the swamp.

'No jumping in,' hissed Benny beside me. 'Remember what happened to Chester.'

'It's not something I'm likely to forget,' I replied grimly.

Major Francis slid slowly down into the swamp until it reached his chest. He began to move forward, holding his rifle above his head to keep the firing mechanism dry.

I went next, my feet sinking into the mud on the bottom. Carefully, I moved through the water in the Major's wake. I hoped there wouldn't be any more pointed bamboo stakes lying in wait for us beneath the murky surface.

Benny looked around suspiciously as we waded along.

'Are there any crocodiles here?' he asked Eddie.

'Not as far as I know,' said Eddie. 'But nothing would surprise me in this place.'

The water in the swamp was so dark and thick that it was impossible to see below the surface. In fact, it was more like runny mud than water. And it stank. All sorts of vegetation had fallen into it and rotted. The smell was awful. I dreaded to think what creatures were lurking there, swimming round my legs.

After two hours of wading through the swamp, we reached a patch of firm ground, a clearing in the trees. Major Francis gestured to us to climb out of the water. As Benny hauled himself out in front of me, I saw that the backs of his arms were a mass of leeches.

'Benny!' I said. 'You've got company.'

Benny looked around, puzzled, and then he realized what I meant. He took one look at his arms and his face turned into an expression of deep revulsion.

'Oh no! Disgusting!' he said. His eyes went to my neck and he said, 'Mind, I'm not the only one.'

I was out of the water by this time. I looked down and saw that I also had leeches sticking to me. Remembering what I'd been told about not pulling them off, I took out a lighter and set light to a piece of twig from a bush. Benny and I took turns to burn the leeches off each other.

While we de-leeched ourselves, Major Francis got Tony to crank up the radio and check in with the other units. No one had anything to report. There was no sign of the enemy. Chester Harris had been the only casualty so far

Suddenly, Mack Mackenzie stiffened.

'What is it?' I asked.

'I saw a movement over there, behind that clump of bushes,' Mack replied in a low voice.

'We'd better tell the Major,' I said.

'The Major's already spotted it,' murmured Major Francis, who'd appeared to come out of nowhere to join us. 'Well done, Mackenzie.'

'Is it the enemy?' I asked, reaching for my rifle.

'I don't think so,' said the Major. 'It's probably some locals who are curious about us. We ought to go and make contact. But not all of us. We don't want to scare them. Fancy coming, Taggart?'

'Yes,' I nodded. 'If they're just locals, shall I bring my rifle?'

The Major gave me a hard look of disapproval.

'When you're on patrol you keep your rifle with you at all times, whatever the situation,' he said. 'Providing you want to stay alive, that is.'

Turning to the rest of the unit, the Major announced, 'I think some locals are watching us. Taggart and I are going to talk to them. It may be a trap, with the Communists using the locals to lure us into it. If we're not back here in three hours, Eddie Kershaw will take over command. Understood, Kershaw?'

'Understood, Major,' nodded Eddie. 'We'll come and find you if you don't come back.'

The Major headed along a path into the jungle with me close behind. Although he still kept glancing from side to side, and up into the leafy canopy of the trees, I got the impression he knew where he was going.

'Been here before, Major?' I asked.

'Yes,' he nodded. 'I was here a year ago. If I'm right these will be the same locals I met then. They're traditionally nomadic hunter-gatherers, but they've taken to growing crops as well. Every year they come back to the same place to farm it. They can grow enough to see them through the rest of the year, while they're on the move.'

Suddenly he put up his hand.

'Stop,' he said, keeping his voice low.

I halted, my rifle ready, just in case.

The Major called out in a language I didn't recognize. Although we'd all had a crash course in the local languages, it didn't sound like any of the words we'd been taught for 'Hello' or 'Friend'.

'I'm calling out the name of the local headman,' the Major explained. 'And the name they call me, which roughly translated means Big Fat Man.'

'Big Fat Man?' I repeated, surprised, looking at the Major. He was hardly what I would describe as being fat. Or indeed big.

The Major gave a smile.

'Compared to the locals, we're all fat. We're also tall, even short people like me.'

Suddenly, so quietly that I hadn't even heard them come through the undergrowth, two dark-skinned men appeared. They were tiny, so small and thin that for a moment I thought they were children. And then I saw their aged faces and realized their size had fooled me briefly. One held a spear, the other a long piece of bamboo. They both looked at me suspiciously.

'Put up your rifle as a sign that we're here in peace,' said the Major. 'But keep it ready just in case the Commies pop up.'

I did as the Major ordered.

The Major stepped forward, head bowed, the palms of his hands together in a form of greeting.

The two locals bowed their heads towards the Major, held out their clasped hands to acknowledge the greeting and gestured us to follow them.

We walked behind them for about half a mile before we came into a large clearing where there was a huge bamboo long house, on stilts of bamboo, with a roof made of palm leaves. It was an amazing thing to find in the middle of this hostile jungle. Some locals were gathered in the clearing. Yet more of them came out of the long house as we arrived.

One man, who looked older than the rest, stood by the bamboo steps leading up to the long house. The Major went up to him. The two men bowed to one another and began a conversation which sounded like gibberish to me. I couldn't understand one word of it, although I could see that the Major and the older man – whom I guessed was the headman – knew one another.

After a few minutes, the headman led the Major towards the smouldering fire in the centre of the clearing. I followed. The fire was inside a circle of stones. The headman mimed for me and the Major to sit beside it.

'We've been invited to lunch,' the Major explained to me.

'We haven't got much time, Major,' I pointed out. 'You told Eddie to come looking for us in three hours.'

'We'll be back before then,' said the Major. 'If we're not, the rest of our unit will join us here and have a damned fine meal! This war isn't just about fighting the enemy, Taggart, it's about winning the hearts and minds of the local people. Becoming their friends. If we refuse to join them in their meal we'll have insulted their hospitality. We have to show these people that we're different from the Commies they meet. The terrorists rule this jungle by fear. We have to show these people we're on their side. So eat up, and enjoy.'

We sat on the ground beside the fire, and the locals joined us. Looking at these tiny people, I felt as if I had travelled back in time a thousand years. They wore very little clothing, just a kind of loincloth hung round their waist. Their hair was decorated: some had it braided, others had leaves and twigs woven through it.

The Major must have known what I was thinking, because he said, 'Don't be fooled by their appearance, Taggart. They may seem primitive, but they have more knowledge about the jungle and how to live off it than you or I could ever hope to learn in a lifetime. The way they use the jungle is very sophisticated: it provides them with everything they need. As they grow up they learn to identify its plants. And not just a few plants, like you did in training, but hundreds. These people don't fear the jungle like we do. They love it. And they live in harmony with it.'

We were given palm leaves as plates and a piece of sharpened twig to spear food from the ashes of the fire. I poked into the ashes and pulled out something charred.

'What is it?' I asked, looking at it suspiciously.

'Whatever they can get hold of,' said the Major, spearing a piece of food himself, tearing it in half and pushing it into his mouth. 'The smaller pieces will be insects of various sorts, but safe to eat. Trust them, these people have been eating like this for thousands of years and they know what's safe to eat and what's not. The bigger pieces will be snake or eel.'

As I munched on the unfamiliar food, I

whispered, 'Are these people the head-hunters you were telling us about?'

The Major nodded.

'Although as far as I know these particular people haven't taken heads for fifty years. They got religion.' He chuckled. 'In fact, I recall someone telling me that the last head they took belonged to the missionary who came to convert them.'

Our meal carried on for nearly an hour, with the Major talking and me just smiling and saying the occasional local word for 'Thank you' whenever someone passed me something to eat.

The two men we'd first met in the jungle came to sit beside me. The one with the long piece of bamboo pointed at my rifle and then at his piece of bamboo. I was puzzled. Was he asking to trade his piece of bamboo for my rifle? If so, he was going to be out of luck. I held on tighter to my rifle to show that it wasn't for exchange, but the man laughed and shook his head. He put one end of the piece of bamboo to his lips and blew, and I realized that the bamboo was hollow and that he was telling me that it was his weapon, a blowpipe. I pointed at it and gave a frown, to show that I was puzzled by it and wondered how it worked.

The man smiled, pulled a long thorn from his loincloth and popped it between his front teeth. He put the blowpipe to his lips, aimed it at a tree, made sure no one was in the way and blew sharply. Then he gestured to me to get up. I followed him to the tree, taking my rifle with me. When we got there, he pointed at the trunk. Sure enough, there was the thorn embedded in it. The man laughed delightedly, plucked the thorn out and put it back in his loincloth. I had to admit, the blowpipe had been astonishingly accurate . . . and deadly silent. I remembered what someone had said about the jungle people putting poison from plants on the tips of thorns and firing them through blowpipes. I bowed to let him see that I admired his skill, and we went back to the fire.

The Major was asking lots of questions. I could tell from the mime and gestures he made that he was asking about the Communist terrorists and where they were in the jungle. The Major asked a question that I could see made the headman look very uncomfortable. The headman was silent for a moment, then he summoned one of the younger men and gave an order. The younger man nodded and headed towards the long house.

'I asked about someone I met last time I was here,' the Major said to me. 'I wanted to know where he was.'

The younger man came down the steps from the long house. Following him was a woman, her head bowed. It was difficult to tell how old she was – she could have been thirty, or even fifty.

The Major stood up as she approached the fire and bowed low to her. She bowed back.

The Major spoke to her quietly and gently, and she replied. Even not knowing the language, I could tell that she was very unhappy and that what she was saying was causing her great distress.

The Major listened to her, nodding all the time. When she had finished, he bowed to her again and said something in the local language.

Next he turned to the headman and

spoke to him. By the tone of his voice the Major was saying something very serious. The headman nodded, understanding. Finally the Major and the headman bowed low to one another, and the Major turned to me.

'Right, Taggart,' he said, 'let's get back to join the rest of the unit before they come looking for us.'

I made my own bow to the locals and mimed my thanks to them for a delicious meal. Then I followed the Major back along the track towards the clearing where our unit were waiting. As we walked, I told him about the man with the blowpipe. He nodded.

'They are superb hunters,' he said. 'Silent and deadly. Even so, a blowpipe doesn't stand much of a chance against machine-guns, no matter how skilled the person using it is.'

'True,' I agreed. Then I added, 'Whatever that woman was telling you, it didn't look like good news.'

'It wasn't,' replied the Major. 'Her husband was a good man. He gave me useful information last time. Not for any reward, but because he was fed up with the terrorists robbing them of the little food they have. It turns out that Chung Lo himself killed him in front of his wife and the rest of the people as a warning against helping us.'

I looked at him, shocked.

'Haven't we just put them back in a dangerous position by having a meal with them?' I asked.

'No,' answered the Major. 'The Communists know that the local custom is to offer food to all visitors, no matter who they are. But telling us where the Communists are hiding is a different matter.'

I frowned, puzzled.

'But surely, when you had that long chat with the headman, he was giving you information?' I said.

The Major nodded.

'Indeed he was,' he acknowledged. 'But not new information; he was only confirming what I already knew.'

'It's the same thing,' I said. 'His people are at risk.'

'They're at risk if we don't defeat the Communist terrorists on this mission,' he said. 'But that's not going to happen. I gave my word to that widow that we will avenge her husband's death. This time we are going to clear these terrorists out once and for all.'

Chapter 8
'THEY'RE ALL DEAD'

As the Major and I walked into the clearing to rejoin the unit, we heard it: the sound of gunfire. It was distant, although it was hard to tell how far away it was because the thick jungle muffled the sound. At the same time the radio crackled and we heard a voice say through crackle and distortion, 'Unit Two under attack. Repeat, Unit Two under attack.'

The voice stopped abruptly, leaving just a hissing and a crackling noise from the radio. But the gunfire carried on.

'I'll go, Major,' said Eddie. To the rest of us he said, 'Two volunteers?'

Benny and I looked at one another and nodded.

'Me and Benny are with you,' I said.

Eddie led the way, moving faster than we had travelled before, his eyes looking ahead, as well as to the left and right of the jungle path. Unit Two were probably about three miles away to our east. Under normal circumstances, over clear terrain, even with the weight of a full pack and weapons, it was a distance that would have taken us thirty minutes. Through this jungle it was going to take us hours.

'We'll use the river in case the path is booby-trapped,' said Eddie. 'It'll also be quicker.'

We slid into the river. The water came up to our waists. The muddy bottom and strong current made progress slow. But it would have been even slower trying to hack our way along the overgrown path. All the time the sound of gunfire continued ahead of us. There were lots of weapons being used, we could tell from the noise. Suddenly, the gunfire stopped and the jungle was eerily quiet. We became aware of the usual noises again – the birds, the chattering of the monkeys up in the trees, the flies and mosquitoes buzzing. In my mind there was one question: who had won, our guys or the enemy?

Checking the compass, we realized the

river was taking us due north. So we climbed out and began hacking our way through the thick jungle, cutting through undergrowth, spending precious minutes untangling ourselves from the sharp thorns of the creeping vines which clung to our clothes. Soon we came to a swamp and carefully entered the stinking stagnant water to wade across it. All the while leeches were attaching themselves to us, but this time we didn't stop to get them off. Ahead of us, our mates were in need of help.

It took us four hours of hard slog to reach the site of the gun battle. As we walked into the clearing where the fight had been, we saw that we were too late. Nine bodies lay around, all dead. Every one of them was from Unit Two.

The sight hit me like a punch in the stomach. Less than twenty-four hours ago we'd all been mates together, laughing and joking, getting ready for action, all in the plane waiting to jump, and now they were all dead. I felt sick: if the terrorists had ambushed Unit One, it could have been me lying there. A cold corpse.

Unit Two's radio set was still on. Through the crackling I could hear Tony Gerson's voice repeating, 'Unit Two, do you read? Over.' There was a click, then Tony's voice repeated the question: 'Unit Two, do you read? Over.'

I hurried over to the radio, picked up the hand microphone, pressed the button to transmit and said, 'This is Trooper Taggart. Nine members of Unit Two dead. Over.'

Tony's voice crackled through the speaker, 'Unit One to Taggart. Please confirm nine dead. Not ten? Over.'

I pressed the transmit button again and said, 'Taggart. Confirm nine deceased. No Commie bodies. Over.'

No bodies of any of the terrorists. Did that mean that none had been killed? No, it was more likely that the terrorists had taken their dead with them.

The radio crackled into life again and Tony's voice said, 'Check for missing unit member and advise. Over and out.'

Eddie began searching the edge of the clearing.

'Careful,' Benny warned. 'They might still be here, waiting to ambush whoever turns up.'

75

As he said it, there was a rustle from some bushes. All three of us snatched up our rifles and aimed them at the spot.

'Whoah! Hold it, mates!' said an English voice. Then Terry Swift from Unit Three stepped into the clearing, with Steve Conway from the same unit behind him.

We put up our guns.

'We came when we heard the gunfire,' said Steve.

He stopped when he saw the dead men from Unit Two dotted around the clearing. The look on his face was one of sheer anger.

'We were too late, eh?' he said bitterly.

'Did you see any sign of the terrorists on the way here?' asked Eddie.

Terry and Steve shook their heads.

'What about one of our own blokes?' I asked, and I explained that we'd only found nine bodies.

Terry and Steve shook their heads again.

'We didn't see anyone,' said Terry.

'We'd better look,' said Benny. 'He may have been wounded and crawled away to hide.'

We searched all round the clearing, but

found nothing. There was no sign of the missing soldier.

Our search revealed blood on leaves and bushes. We guessed it was from the enemy. If we were right, it meant that some of them had been wounded in the gun battle. There were also marks to show that things had been dragged through the undergrowth. Presumably the enemy had taken their dead and wounded with them, pulling them along behind in their haste to leave.

By now Terry and Steve had checked the name tags on the bodies to identify the dead men.

'It's Denny Jones who's missing,' said Terry. 'If he's not around here, he's probably still alive and with the Communists.'

'Why have they taken him?' asked Benny.

'As a hostage,' said Eddie.

'Well, let's go after them,' said Terry. 'The sooner we catch up with them, the sooner we can free Denny.'

'We don't know which way they've gone,' Benny pointed out.

'There are some clues,' said Eddie. 'We didn't pass them on our way in from the west. And Steve and Terry didn't see them either when they came in from the east. So that rules out them going either east or west.'

'They could have been hiding in the jungle and we passed them,' suggested Benny.

'It's possible,' nodded Eddie, 'but the number of men it would have taken to wipe out almost the whole of Unit Two means it's a pretty large outfit. Possibly twenty of them, maybe more. That big an outfit is difficult to hide. Especially if they're carrying dead and wounded. And taking Denny with them as a prisoner.'

'So, if none of us passed them, they either went south or north,' said Steve.

'The blood and flattened undergrowth is on the northern side of this clearing. Was that done deliberately, to make us think they are going that way, when they're really going south? Or are they really going north?'

'They won't be heading south,' said Terry. 'If they did they'd soon be out in the open. They'll want to use the cover of the jungle.'

'I reckon they'll be heading north,

towards their HQ in the heart of the jungle,' I said.

The others nodded in agreement.

'North it is, then,' said Eddie.

Steve indicated the dead men.

'What about them,' he said. 'Shouldn't we bury them?'

'We'll come back later and do it,' said Eddie. 'The more time we spend here, the longer we give the terrorists to get away. We need to get after them quickly. I'll tell the Major what we're doing.'

Eddie picked up the hand mike on the radio set, clicked the transmit button and said, 'Kershaw to Unit One. Do you read? Over.'

The response was immediate. Tony Gerson's voice crackled through the speakers: 'Unit One reading you. Over.'

'We have re-formed Unit Two with additional personnel from Unit Three,' reported Eddie. 'Shall proceed in pursuit of enemy. Over.'

Then we heard Major Francis's voice asking, 'Any sign of missing unit member?'

'Negative,' replied Eddie. 'We believe he is a prisoner of the terrorists.'

The Major's voice came back, 'Message

received and understood, Unit Two. Keep in touch. Over and out.'

And that was it. The five of us were now Unit Two: Me, Eddie, Benny, Steve and Terry. Stepping into dead men's shoes. And half the strength of the original unit.

'Can you carry the radio for the first stretch, Benny?' asked Eddie. 'We'll take turns as we go.'

Benny nodded.

'Leave it to me,' he said, hoisting the radio up and looping the strap over his shoulder.

'OK,' said Eddie. 'Let's go.'

Chapter 9
IN PURSUIT

When you track people you have to be sharp-eyed. All the time you're looking for signs showing the direction in which they went. Grass trodden flat. Bushes with branches and twigs broken. Fallen leaves disturbed. Squashed insects. Broken spider webs.

In a damp environment like the jungle, footprints show up in the earth. They can reveal an awful lot about your 'prey'. Is one footprint deeper than the other? If so, your prey is limping. Are the prints deep? If so, it means the person may be carrying something heavy. In which case they'll be going slower than you. If you find a slope, the chances are there'll be the skid mark of a foot on it.

Prints tell you a story. You can work out how long ago they were made, so you can tell how far ahead of you your prey is. Check how many different sorts of footprint there are. This will tell you how many people are in the party you are pursuing. The length between the footprints will give you an idea of how fast they are travelling. Are the prints barefoot, or are they wearing shoes? If shoes, what sort of shoes? Army issue, or civilian?

Even if the person you are hunting uses the rivers and swamps to avoid leaving footprints, sooner or later they have to get out on to dry land. When they do, they leave marks by the water's edge: scratches and tears in the mud, broken branches.

All this helps build up a picture of the quarry – the people you are chasing after. We had already decided that there were a lot of them and that they were heavily armed, because they'd almost wiped out Unit Two. I wondered what sort of condition Denny Jones was in. Had he been wounded? Was he still alive?

'If they're carrying their wounded – perhaps even their dead – they'll be travelling slowly,' Eddie pointed out. 'They'll know we'll be after them, and catching up.'

'So they'll have an ambush waiting for us somewhere along the way,' said Steve.

Eddie nodded.

'An ambush or booby-traps. Maybe both. So keep your eyes and ears peeled. If you hear anything out of the ordinary, dive flat and fire.'

We began our trek northwards through the jungle, following the trail probably taken by the terrorists.

Assuming they were carrying their wounded comrades, they would keep out of rivers and swamps. That made it easier for us, because we could follow their trail by the tell-tale signs they had left, like crushed plants and snapped branches.

The main thing we watched out for were booby-traps. You can make a mantrap from bamboo quite easily, using the natural strength of the wood as its spring. Cover the trap with leaves. When it's trodden on, the trap is sprung and the bamboo 'jaws' of sharpened stakes snap together, gripping your leg in a painful lock.

And it's not just at ground level that you can run into dangerous booby-traps. A heavy weight, such as a log or a rock, can be tied to a tree by a length of vine, with a trigger hidden down on the trail. Knock the trigger and the weight is dislodged, swinging down from the tree on the vine and crushing your skull.

Luckily we didn't encounter any of these. At the back of our minds we had the image of Chester Harris impaled on the sharpened bamboo stakes in the swamp, so we knew what the Communists were capable of.

We took turns to carry the radio, and also to take point. Eddie had taken point for the first half mile, then Terry, then it was my turn.

I was just moving along the trail to overtake Terry to take point, when I heard a metallic click ahead. A rifle bolt.

'Down!' I yelled.

Immediately we threw ourselves flat on the ground. Just in time, because there was a burst of gunfire from a clump of bushes ahead and tracers of bullets whistled over our heads.

I levelled my M1 and fired at the bushes. I was aware of Eddie beside me. He'd scrambled to his knees and was firing round after round in the same direction.

Benny, Steve and Terry had also fired into the bushes. They were now on their feet, crouched low, swinging their rifles round at the rest of the jungle surrounding us, ready to fire at the slightest sound or movement.

There was no more firing.

'Stay back in case it's a trick,' said Eddie. 'I'll check it out.'

Cautiously, Eddie moved forwards towards the clump of bushes, finger on the trigger of his rifle.

He reached the bushes and checked the ground behind them. Then he gestured for us to move forwards

'It's OK,' he said. 'There's only one of them.'

'Is he dead?' called Benny.

Eddie nodded.

''The amount of bullets we hit him with, he didn't have a chance.'

I joined the others and we looked down at the dead terrorist. His rifle lay beside him.

'Why only one?' asked Terry, puzzled. 'He can't have expected to shoot all of us.'

'That wasn't his job,' said Eddie. 'His job

was to keep us pinned down so the rest of them could get away. Maybe shoot one or two of us, if he could. But he knew the chances were that he wasn't going to get away alive. It was a suicide mission. He was a brave man, even if he was fighting for the other side. Luckily for us, thanks to Ian's sharp ears, he didn't hold us at bay for as long as they'd hoped.'

We radioed to Major Francis about our encounter with the lone terrorist, to warn Unit One in case there were other ambushes waiting for them. Then we moved on.

Chapter 10
RIVER AMBUSH

For the next two miles we followed in the enemy's footsteps through the under-growth. We continued to keep our eyes and ears alert for any booby-traps or for another ambush.

Following behind the Communists meant we didn't have to hack at the vegetation with our machetes to make a path for ourselves: they'd already done it for us.

All the time I was aware of the jungle closing in on us, the tendrils of the vines snatching at our clothing as we passed, the drip drip drip of the water dropping on us from the leaves. And always there were the sounds of the chattering birds and monkeys high above us, and all sorts of other creatures rasping and munching and scrabbling all around.

We came upon one vicious booby-trap the Communists had left lying for us: a bamboo mantrap hidden beneath leaves. Steve thought the pile of leaves looked suspicious, so he prodded it with a stick. The jaws of the trap sprang together so hard they broke the stick in half.

'That could have been one of our legs,' Benny commented.

Finally we came to a river. It was about fifty yards to the opposite bank.

Eddie held up his hand and stopped us moving out of the undergrowth.

'If there's going to be a big ambush, this is where it will be,' he said. 'They'll be hidden on the other side of the river.'

We crouched down and got out our binoculars and focused on the vegetation on the other bank. Although I couldn't see any sign of movement, I could see the scrapes and marks in the mud on the river bank where the Communists had climbed out of the water.

'What do we do?' whispered Terry. 'We can't just stay here. For all we know there may be no one at all lying in wait for us.'

'The only answer is to get across the

river somewhere else and work our way round behind them,' I suggested.

'Me and Ian can do that, while you lot stay here and keep watch,' said Benny.

'OK,' nodded Eddie. 'But take care crossing. If they see you, they'll shoot. And there are not many hiding places when you're in the middle of a river.'

'We'll try to find a bend to hide us from their view,' I said.

'Be careful crossing at a bend,' warned Eddie. 'The current's much faster there. And it's flowing this way. So if you fall you'll be swept back, right into their firing line.'

'Don't worry,' I said. 'I intend to stay alive.'

'You know what would be good?' said Benny. 'A diversion.'

'What sort of diversion?' asked Terry.

'Well, we're going towards the left. The Commies might see the vegetation moving and guess that's the way we're heading. If one of you blokes went off to the right first, making sure you shook the bushes and banged into branches –'

'They'd see them moving and start shooting,' finished Steve.

'No, they won't,' said Eddie. 'They'll wait, hoping to pick us off when we're halfway across the river. Good thinking, Benny. I'll set off to the right, making sure they can see the direction I'm going in. Give me ten seconds before you and Ian creep off the other way, keeping as out of sight as you can.'

We nodded.

Eddie moved off to the right, keeping parallel with the river, shaking branches as he went to divert the enemy's attention.

Benny and I moved off into the undergrowth to our left, crouching low and doing our best not to disturb the vegetation as we moved.

After half a mile we found a bend in the river which hid us from the enemy. As Eddie had warned us, here at the bend the river ran much faster.

'Excellent,' said Benny. 'The perfect crossing place.'

'It looks deep in the middle,' I said.

'The Commies got across it, so it can't be that deep,' said Benny.

'That was back there,' I pointed out. 'The current is faster here, so it'll be deeper.'

Benny nudged me and pointed to a fallen tree trunk.

'There's our transport,' he said. 'One, it'll hold us up as we cross. Two, if we do get swept into their line of fire, it'll give us cover.'

Benny and I set to work and dragged the tree trunk to the edge of the river. As we came out of the undergrowth at the water's edge, I half expected a hail of bullets from the opposite bank, but none came. Whether that meant the terrorists hadn't come this far, or whether it meant they would wait for us to get to the middle of the river before firing at us, we were about to find out.

We pushed the tree trunk into the water and slowly slipped in alongside it. Keeping our rifles out of the water with one hand, and clinging on to the floating tree trunk with the other, we began our way across the river. At first the water was at waist height, then at chest height, then at neck height and, finally, we were floating, kicking out for the opposite bank. Now it was much more difficult to stop the tree trunk from heading downriver with the current, but with both of us kicking hard we managed to reach the shallows and felt mud beneath our feet again.

We had made it. We jammed the trunk between some roots to stop it floating away. If we needed to get back across the river in an emergency, it would provide cover.

We hauled ourselves out of the river and dumped all our equipment, except our rifles and ammunition and some grenades, on the ground and covered them with palm leaves to hide them. If we were going to make a surprise attack, sneaking up on the enemy from behind, I didn't want to do it weighed down with a rucksack.

Then we set off through the undergrowth, moving as silently as we could. I thought of the Malays and how they had appeared in front of the Major and me as if out of thin air. Invisible: that's how I wanted it to be when I came up against the Communists. I wondered if there was even an ambush lying in wait for us.

There was.

Benny heard them before I did. It was just a tiny cough, but it was enough. We froze in our positions, and then moved through the undergrowth, very slowly, inch by inch, stopping all the time to scan the ground ahead, barely breathing, we were so intent on not making any sound that would attract the enemy's attention. Our lives depended on it.

I glimpsed them beneath some low-growing palm leaves. There were six of them, all with automatic rifles. Their attention was fixed on the opposite bank of the river, where Eddie, Terry and Steve were. The three guys were doing a good job of keeping the terrorists' attention: every now and then a branch would move, or a bush would shudder. At once the Communists would raise their rifles to fire, then lower them again when no one appeared. Eddie was right: they were waiting for us to get into the river and start to wade across.

I looked at Benny and held up six fingers. He nodded, because he had already counted them. I pointed at myself, indicating that I would take the three on the left. Benny nodded; he'd take the others.

Benny raised three fingers in a countdown: three . . . two . . . one . . .

93

We both leaped to our feet and started firing, fingers glued to the triggers, bullets pouring out in a hail of ear-splitting noise and fire.

Two of the terrorists went down straight away. The others tried to turn and shoot at us, but they didn't have a chance.

Benny and I stopped firing.

I stepped through the undergrowth to the edge of the river and waved my rifle.

Eddie, Terry and Steve came into view on the other bank and waved back. Then they began to wade across the river, Steve carrying the radio.

'I'll go and get my stuff,' said Benny.

'I'll pick mine up after the boys get here,' I said. 'Just in case there's anyone else lying in wait for us.'

Benny nodded and hurried back the way we'd come to collect his rucksack and equipment.

As I watched Eddie, Steve and Terry reach the middle of the river safely, I thought of the Malay woman the Major and I had met. The one whose husband had been killed. I looked down at the six dead Communists and whispered, 'He's been partly avenged. But there's still a lot to do if we're going to get the rest of you.'

And that was when I heard the sound of gunfire to my left.

Chapter 11
DEADLY ENCOUNTER

Unlike when we'd heard the gunfire that had wiped out Unit Two, this was only a short burst. The sound came from the west, which meant that Major Francis and Unit One were involved.

Terry was already cranking up the radio.

'Unit One, this is Unit Two, do you read? Over,' he said into the mike.

First there were only crackles and hisses, then Tony Gerson's voice came through.

'Unit Two, Unit One reading you. Over.'

'Unit One, we heard sounds of shooting from your direction. Over.'

'Unit Two, our situation contained. Enemy personnel curtailed. No casualties taken. What's your situation? Over.'

Enemy personnel curtailed. They'd come

up against some of the Communists and killed them.

Terry spoke into the hand mike.

'Our situation successful. Six enemy personnel curtailed.'

'Tell them we're making camp for the night,' said Eddie. 'Will continue pursuit at dawn.'

Terry passed that message over the radio.

'Confirmed. Making camp also. Over and out.'

In the heat of the chase I'd almost forgotten that night was coming. Maybe it was because the jungle was dark anyway, with the trees keeping out the light.

We set to work with our machetes, cutting lengths of bamboo and lashing them together with vines to make platforms to sleep on.

'We'll take turns to keep watch,' said Eddie. 'One hour at a time.'

'I'll take first watch,' I volunteered quickly, before anyone else could speak.

Eddie nodded and started making a rota of the others.

My reason for volunteering to take first watch was because, after the excitement of the day's events, I was pretty sure I wouldn't be able to get to sleep easily. This way my adrenalin could wind down while I sat quietly on the look-out. Also, there's nothing worse than being woken up to go on watch and then trying to get to sleep an hour later.

While the other guys settled down, I sat with my rifle in my hands, my eyes searching the darkness of the jungle and my ears alert for any sounds other than the usual ones from the insects and animals.

Even though it was night, the air was still hot and humid.

I had made myself a little bamboo platform, supported on tree roots, to raise me off the ground. I didn't fancy being attacked by a load of insects getting into my shorts while I was sitting keeping guard.

I sat there and thought about what had happened that day: Chester Harris speared on the bamboo spikes; Unit Two virtually wiped out; Denny Jones captured; the first ambush by the lone terrorist; and the six terrorists we'd killed by the river. It had been a long, eventful day.

The image of our nine men from Unit Two lying dead in the clearing haunted me. I'd seen dead people before, but not in such numbers. Once again the thought that it could so easily have been me and the rest of Unit One lying dead hit me.

I also thought of Denny Jones. I hadn't really known him at all; he'd just been one of the other ninety-nine men in training at the camp at Singapore. I wondered if he was still alive. Had he been injured? How were the enemy treating him? I wondered how I would feel if that had happened to me; if I'd been taken prisoner by the enemy, after they'd killed all the rest of my mates in front of me.

I strained my ears, listening, but all I could hear were the buzzing insects and the sound of the river nearby.

Next morning we were all up at dawn. We made breakfast from our rations – not like what we got at home, or even in camp, but it gave us the energy to get back on the trail.

We made radio contact with Unit One, confirming that we were continuing in pursuit of the Communists.

Each unit had been working in a line towards the centre of the jungle – like the spokes on a wheel, as Major Francis had put it – and now those spokes were getting closer to the central hub, we were getting nearer to the units on either side of us. We calculated that we were about two miles away from Unit One, to our west, and Unit Three, to our east. Our circle was slowly but surely closing on the terrorists' HQ.

'The nearer we get to them, and the tighter our circle moves in, the more chance there is they'll try to break through our lines,' Major Francis said over the radio. 'Keep a close watch out for a counter-attack.'

We packed up our equipment and set off, moving in single file. It was my turn to carry the radio first, so I went in the middle, with Eddie at point, Terry second, and Benny and Steve behind me, keeping watch in case we were attacked from the rear.

When you're on patrol in enemy territory, you don't just keep looking ahead all the time, you have to keep watching behind you, as well as from side to side.

The jungle was as thick as ever. To keep up speed, we used streams much of the time, our senses on alert for an ambush or a booby-trap.

During the march, we took turns at carrying the radio, taking point and bringing up the rear.

After three hours we'd travelled probably no more than a mile. This would have been slow going anywhere else, but in jungle as thick as this it was quite a fast rate.

An hour later, things changed. We'd just hauled ourselves through some swamp and were pushing along a track, overgrown with vegetation, when Terry, on point, suddenly gave a yell.

'It's Denny!'

With that, Terry hurried forwards. I could just make out the shape of a body lying face down. The only thing I could see clearly was a pair of regulation army boots poking into the path.

'Wait!' called Eddie, who was bringing up the rear. *'Don't touch him!'*

'I've got to see if he's alive,' said Terry impatiently. He knelt down beside the body and lifted Denny to turn him over.

'NO!!' bellowed Eddie.

I turned to look at Eddie, surprised by the urgency in his shout. He was trying to get past Benny, who was hampered by the weight of the radio. Then there was the sound of an explosion and I was thrown backwards by the force of the blast, landing in the undergrowth.

I staggered to my feet and saw Terry collapsed over what was left of Denny, his clothing blackened and covered in blood.

Eddie hurried to Terry. He examined him quickly, then shook his head grimly.

'He's dead,' he said.

'What happened?' asked Steve.

'They booby-trapped Denny's body,' said Eddie. 'It looks like they put three grenades with the pins nearly out beneath him. As soon as anyone moved him, the pins came out and the grenades went off. They probably even shortened the fuses of the grenades so whoever picked Denny up didn't stand a chance.'

'You knew?' I asked.

Eddie shrugged.

'I guessed,' he said. 'That's why I shouted. I saw the same thing happen when I was in Burma. Everything's a possible booby-trap in the jungle, even your mate's dead body.'

He shook his head.

'Better get on the radio and report it to the Major,' he said to Benny. 'Denny Jones found dead, plus one new casualty, Trooper Terry Swift.'

Benny cranked up the radio and passed the message on. Eddie took the ID tags off the bodies, put them in his pocket and we moved on again. We were getting closer to the enemy, and the nearer we got, the more dangerous it became.

Chapter 12
THE CIRCLE CLOSES

We continued further into the dark heart of the jungle for another two hours. During that time there was no sign of the Communists.

'Maybe they got past us?' suggested Benny. 'Maybe they really are heading out of the jungle?'

Eddie shook his head.

'No chance. We've been getting closer and closer to the other units. One of us would have spotted something, or come up against someone. No, we're pushing them into the centre.'

'Then why aren't they fighting back?' asked Steve, puzzled. 'It's just been the occasional ambush so far.'

'Because they're guerrillas,' said Eddie. 'That's the way guerrillas work. You don't have a stand-up, face-to-face battle; you make a sneak attack and then withdraw.'

'Even so, I still don't understand why they're letting us push them into a corner like this,' I put in.

Just then we heard a sound to our left and we whirled round, rifles pointed, fingers poised on triggers, but it was Mack Mackenzie from our old Unit One.

'I guessed that was you blokes,' he said. 'Nattering away like a bunch of old women!'

'Old women who nearly shot you,' said Benny, lowering the barrel of his rifle.

'No chance!' grinned Mack.

'What's the latest?' asked Eddie.

'The rest of Unit One are just back there,' said Mack. 'We've made contact with Unit Ten on our other side. We're all coming together in a big circle, a big armed ring right round the Commies.'

'How far away are they?' I asked.

'From what we can work out, only about two or three miles. The Major's looking for volunteers to carry out a night observation patrol to find out what sort of defences they've got round their HQ. He wants reports back from four directions so we've got all the angles covered.'

'I'll go,' I said.

'And me,' said Eddie.

'Me too,' said Benny.

'Count me in as well,' added Steve.

'Two men only to each patrol, the Major said,' Mack told us with a rueful shrug. 'He reckons any more than that will cause too much noise and alert the Commies. Sorry, guys, but fair's fair, it's got to be the first two: Ian and Eddie. The rest of us are to wait in camp. We'll put together a plan of attack after we get the reports from the patrols.'

'Any news on Chester?' asked Benny.

'Yes,' nodded Mack. 'Pete and Bill got him into a chopper. At the last count he was still alive, but he's going to be out of action for quite a while. One of the bamboo stakes went right into his belly. He's going to need surgery.'

'And Pete and Bill?' I asked.

'They caught up with us,' said Mack. 'So, it looks like the whole gang is back together.' Then he remembered about Unit Two being hit, and Denny and Terry, and he added apologetically, 'Well, almost the whole gang.' But he brightened up again and said, 'Anyway, make up your camp and then come and join the rest of the boys. We can swap notes. I'll go tell the Major you two are doing the night patrol.'

With that, Mack left to join the rest of Unit One.

So, we'd finally joined up with everyone again. We were back together – or, at least, the survivors were. One big ring round the terrorists' HQ. And tonight, I'd be going into that ring.

I was glad that I was going on the night patrol with Eddie. Out of all of us, apart from the Major himself, Eddie knew so much more about surviving against an enemy in the jungle. He wouldn't have been caught on the bamboo stakes like Chester Harris, or been killed by the booby-trapped body like Terry. He'd realized their mistakes, but his warnings came too late.

While the rest of the guys set up our camp, I asked him about the patrol.

'How are we going to see? This jungle is dark enough during daylight hours. We're not going to see *anything* at night.'

Eddie shook his head.

'There's no such thing as total darkness when you're outside,' he said, 'even in thick jungle like this. You have to take time for your eyes to get accustomed to it. You find a spot that appears totally black, and you sit and look, getting your eyes used to it. Your eyes change, just like a cat's, or any other animal that hunts in the night. The pupil of your iris opens wider, letting more light into the back of your eye. And there is light of sorts. Light from the moon. Light reflecting off the swamp water. Off the leaves of the palm trees. Not much, but it's there. You adapt to it, and you'll be surprised how much you can see.

'The main thing is to move slowly. Very slowly. You don't want any sudden surprises. You test every inch in front of you before you move. And keep silent. Absolutely no talking. If you want to tell me something, use sign language. Hand up for 'Stop'. Hand down for 'Get down'. If you see a group, hold up a finger for every person you see in it. We'll be near enough to read each other's signals. Providing you don't try any complicated sort of signals. Make your signals easy to understand, that's the main thing.

'And one more thing. If you come up

against any of the enemy and have to take them out, use a silent weapon. A knife. Your hands. We don't want to start shooting and alert the rest. OK?'

I nodded.

'OK,' said Eddie. He looked around at the fading light. 'We'll move off now. By the time we get to our objective, it'll be dark.'

As we started, taking only our rifles and knives with us, and a water bottle strapped to each belt, Eddie said, 'Oh, one more thing: remember, if *you* can see in the dark, so can the enemy. Like I said, keep it very slow. No noises. If we're caught, we're dead. And so will be this mission.'

With that thought, we began to work our way slowly along a track towards the enemy HQ.

Chapter 13
NIGHT PATROL

I guessed the track had been made by the terrorists to help them move around the jungle. Eddie was right about the light. When my eyes had adjusted to the darkness, I was able to see with a clearness that amazed me. We made our way along the rough and winding track on hands and knees, feeling our way with our hands in case of booby-traps. Each time I searched in front of me, I wondered if I was going to set something off. I was always on the alert, ready to leap back if I heard any sound that might be a trap going off to snap my probing fingers.

Eddie was taking most of the risk, being at the front, but he knew what he was doing. Suddenly he stopped crawling and his hand flapped in a 'Get down' gesture. Immediately I lay flat. Eddie held up two fingers: two Communists were directly ahead, probably a look-out post for their HQ.

Eddie gestured towards the swamp, just a few yards away from the track. Pointing to where young bamboo shoots were growing at the base of a tree, he pulled out his knife and sawed silently at one of the shoots. He held the cut-off shoot towards me to show me the length he wanted me to cut for myself. While I cut a shoot, Eddie cleaned out the pith from the centre of his shoot, until he had a hollow tube. I did the same.

Eddie now put one end of the bamboo tube in his mouth and indicated water going over his head.

I got the message. We were going to bypass the guards using the swamp, keeping under the stagnant water by breathing through the hollowed-out bamboo shoots. I thought of the leeches and all the other things in that water, and my skin crawled. Say a leech got into a nostril? They were noted for getting into any orifice. The only thing I could do was to be ready to pinch my nose if I felt anything and keep it out.

Eddie took off his shirt and wrapped it round his rifle to help stop it getting clogged up while we were under the water. I did the same. Then we eased ourselves into the stinking water of the swamp. I put one end of the bamboo tube in my mouth and then let myself sink down until the water closed over my head.

It was impossible to see anything. It was a case of working our way forwards by touch. I reached out to Eddie, and he tapped my hand to confirm that we were ready to move forwards. We set off, crawling slowly so as not to make ripples and disturb the water. All the time I was aware that I had to keep low, keep my head below the surface, just in case the guards were watching the swamp. At one point I must have got down too low, because there was the foul taste of putrid water in my mouth as the end of the bamboo tube dropped below the surface.

I lifted my head a fraction and blew out gently, and kept breathing out. When I thought the tube was clear of the water, I took a chance and breathed in. Although I got some more of the water in my mouth, there was air as well.

I kept edging forwards, working my way through the swamp water, until I bumped up against Eddie in front of me. He tapped me on the top of my head. For a second I wasn't sure whether his signal meant me to go down deeper or to get up. Then I felt his shoulders rising up in the water.

I lifted my head cautiously until my mouth was clear of the surface of the swamp. I looked around. Eddie lifted his hand out of the water and gave a thumbs-up sign. We had got past the guards.

I was now aware of a dim reddish glow of camp fires ahead of us in the jungle. I pointed towards it and Eddie nodded: he'd seen it too.

We carried on moving through the swamp, keeping low with just our heads above the water's surface. All the time the reddish glow was getting brighter.

Eddie pointed towards the bank on the other side of the swamp, in the direction of the reddish glow. We moved over to it and heaved ourselves silently out of the water, bringing our wrapped-up rifles with us.

We crawled noiselessly through the undergrowth, stopping just before we came to a large clearing. What I saw there stunned me. I had been expecting some kind of rough camp set up by Chung Lo and his fellow Communists, perhaps with barricades made of bamboo. Instead, what was in front of us was a small village lit by fires, with four long houses on stilts and four small huts, also on stilts, where I guessed supplies were stored.

Machine-gun posts had been set up round the village, each manned by two Communists. The terrorists had obviously turned this village into their HQ. This was why they hadn't attempted to break out. They knew that so long as they hid among the villagers – families with women and children – they were safe from direct attack. We wouldn't risk an all-out assault that could lead to the death of many Malay families.

I made a mental note of the layout of the village: where the long houses and huts were, where the machine-gun posts had been set. I knew that Eddie was doing the same. We spent about an hour just watching the village; watching the movements of the people, both the villagers and the Communists, counting numbers. To get a really accurate picture of how many terrorists and villagers there were, and what the weapon strength inside the village was, we should have spent some of the daylight hours observing, when the village was awake and active. But to do that would be too risky. We would just have to return to the Major with the information we'd been able to gather, add it to the reports from the three other patrols and devise a course of action. One thing was for sure, with so many villagers about, finishing the terrorists off wasn't going to be easy.

Chapter 14

CAPTURED

Eddie and I returned to our camp the same way we had come: using the bamboo tubes to breathe under the swamp water to get past the guards, and then working our way on our hands and knees along the rough track.

Major Francis was waiting for us when we arrived.

'Well?' he asked.

We told him about the village and the risks of launching an all-out attack. We added that there were enemy outposts on the approaches to the village that would be difficult to get past without raising an alarm.

The Major nodded as he listened to what we told him.

'That adds up,' he said. 'I've got a report back from the two men who carried out the observation patrol to the east which bears out what you two saw. Well done. Did you see any sign of a man who might be their leader?'

'This Chung Lo?' I asked.

'Yes,' replied the Major.

I shook my head.

'No,' I said. 'Though at that time of night he might be asleep. I didn't see anyone who looked as if they were giving orders.'

'Me neither,' said Eddie.

'OK,' said the Major. 'Right now you'd both better get some of that muck off you and grab some rest.'

Eddie and I must have been a weird sight: covered in swamp slime from the top of our heads down to our boots. As we were surrounded by swamp with more of the same mucky water, there wasn't much point in going in to try to wash it off. Instead, I grabbed some leaves and used them to scrape off as much of the muck as I could, and then thought: what the hell! I'll have a good bath when this is all over.

Next I took my rifle apart and gave it a good clean. If I was woken up in a hurry I didn't want my rifle jamming on me because it was clogged up.

With my rifle cleaned and its strap looped over an arm – just in case anyone tried to snatch it from me while I was asleep – I clambered on to one of the raised palm-leaf-covered platforms. Eddie had already cleaned his rifle and he was fast asleep.

I closed my eyes and let myself drift off. It was reassuring to know that I was surrounded by the rest of the guys in case there was a surprise attack.

I woke up five hours later. It was the longest I'd slept for a long time. Eddie was already up and he was peeling off the dried muck from the swamp.

'You should have woken me,' I said.

'Why?' said Eddie. 'You needed the sleep. Rest is the best healer when you're in combat. Your body will tell you when it's had enough.'

Benny saw that I was awake and came over, a big grin on his face.

'So,' he said, 'the sleeping beauty's awake.'

'Yes, and while you were snoring away

last night, Eddie and I were up to our necks in swamp water.'

'True,' admitted Benny. To Eddie, he said, 'Have you told him about Greg and Sammy?'

Eddie shook his head.

'Not yet,' he said.

From the tone of Benny's voice, I knew that something was wrong.

'What's happened?' I asked.

'Greg and Sammy were the two blokes from Unit Five who went out on patrol last night. They were checking out the north side of the HQ. Only they never came back.'

'So, either they're dead or the Commies caught them,' said Eddie.

I let Eddie's words sink in, and they made me feel sick. If they'd been caught, then the Communists would be trying to find out information from them about what we were doing. And having seen how these terrorists operated, they wouldn't be doing it in any gentlemanly way.

'We've got to go and rescue them,' I said.

'We will,' said Benny. 'But we can't just

119

go charging in like the Seventh Cavalry. If we do, the villagers and their kids will get caught in the cross-fire between us and the Commies. We've got to use our heads.'

'The Major says we're going to attack tonight,' said Eddie. 'All units. There's a chance the Communists may have forced Greg and Sammy to show them how they got to the HQ. If so, that means whatever route they took from the north is too risky to try again. Which leaves the three ways to the HQ that we used without being caught: south, east and west.'

'Now they've caught Greg and Sammy, they'll be watching every way in and out, not just the northerly route,' I pointed out. 'They'll be doubling up on guards at the outposts.'

Eddie nodded.

'That's what the rest of us think as well,' he said. 'So tonight, when there are more of us, and we go for our underwater midnight swim through the swamp, we're going to take out the sentries at that outpost we saw.'

'If any shooting starts, they'll hear it at the HQ,' I said.

'We hope there won't be any shooting,' said Benny. 'The plan is to put the guards out of action quickly and silently.'

'Doggo and Jim found an outpost on the eastern side, and Desi and Mark got past one on the west,' added Eddie. 'So we're aiming to take them out as well.'

'What about the northern side?' I asked. 'The place where Greg and Sammy got caught?'

'We're leaving them alone. Units Five and Six are going to keep the northern area covered. The plan is that if we push the Commies out of their HQ, they'll run to the north, straight into the blokes from Five and Six.'

'And the villagers?' I asked.

'That's the point of us going in at night,' said Benny. 'We're going to see if we can creep into the village, get into the long houses and get the villagers out to safety, before we attack.'

'Sounds a good plan in theory,' I said.

Eddie laughed.

'All plans are good in theory,' he said. 'The truth is, when they're put into practice, Sod's Law comes into action.'

'What's Sod's Law?' asked Benny.

'What can go wrong will go wrong,' said Eddie. 'Believe me, boys, tonight's mission has all the marks of a disaster waiting to happen. All we can do is our best and hope to salvage as much out of it as we can.'

Chapter 15
ATTACK

Based on the reports that all the patrols had brought back the previous night, it had been decided to use the swamps and rivers to get past the guard outposts into the village, travelling underwater if necessary. Once past the outposts, some men would double back, like we had, and kill the guards.

Our patrol combined the old Unit One and the new Unit Two. The other units had teamed up too and were making their own way to the terrorists' HQ. Units Three and Four were working together, as were Seven and Eight, and Nine and Ten, with Units Five and Six waiting to the north, ready to take on the Communists if they retreated from their HQ. They could also be called in to attack, if needed.

As dusk turned to night, our unit set off. We let our eyes get used to the dark. Then, in a line, our rifles wrapped up, we got into the swamp. As Eddie and I had done this journey before, we led the way. We made sure every man had made himself a bamboo breathing tube for the underwater part of the route.

Our progress was even slower than the previous night, for two reasons: firstly, there were ten of us instead of just two; secondly, because Greg and Sammy had been caught, we expected the guards to be more alert – which meant we had to be extra careful.

Eddie stopped at the same point as the night before when he'd spotted the enemy's outpost. By tapping each other on the shoulder all the way down along the line, we passed the message back for everyone to get underwater. Knowing what a mouthful of swamp water was like, I'd made sure that everyone's breathing tube was really long so that no one else ended up swallowing it.

Last night had shown us how long we had to spend underwater to make sure we got past the enemy guards: three minutes.

I began counting as I moved slowly forward: one . . . two . . . three . . . It seemed to take an eternity before I got to 170 and was able to count those last ten seconds: 171 . . . 172 . . . 173 . . . 174 . . . 175 . . . 176 . . . 177 . . . 178 . . . 179 . . . 180.

At last I let my head come up until I felt the surface of the water lap against the bridge of my nose. I opened my eyes and I turned to look back towards the terrorists' outpost, keeping moving all the time to allow Benny, who was just behind me, room to surface. Finally we all had our heads poking out of the swamp, but we kept the rest of our bodies below the waterline, just in case.

Pete Shaw, Bill Stevens, Jack Roberts and Tony Gerson had volunteered to deal with the guards. They clawed their way out of the swamp. The rest of us – me, Eddie, Benny, Steve Conway, Mack and the Major – carried on through the swamp, getting nearer at every step to the enemy's HQ. All the time I was waiting for a shot to ring out from behind us when one of the enemy sentries saw our guys, but there was no sound from that direction.

As before, I saw the reddish glow from fires ahead of us as we got nearer to the village. We moved closer to the edge of the swamp, working our way along it in single file, keeping close to the bank, crouched low in the water, using the overhanging trees for cover.

Finally we arrived at the spot where Eddie and I had got out of the swamp the night before and observed the Communists' HQ. Eddie and I gestured to the others to get out. Once we were on the land we began uncovering our rifles, making sure they were ready for action.

As we were doing this, there was movement in the swamp behind us and Bill, Jack, Pete and Tony appeared. They gave a thumbs-up sign to let us know that the guards had been dealt with, then they clambered out of the swamp to join us.

The Major now took the lead, moving into an observation position behind some bushes from where he could look into the clearing without being seen. The rest of us joined him, spreading out in a line, hidden in the undergrowth.

The village was the same as the

previous night, except for two large bamboo X-frames in the centre of the clearing. Tied to each one were the bodies of Greg and Sammy. From this distance it was hard to tell if they were unconscious or dead. I used my binoculars to try to get a better view of them. Their heads hung down, so I couldn't see their faces. However, one of them lifted his head for the merest fraction of a second, before dropping it down again. One of them, at least, was still alive.

The Major looked at Eddie, me, Benny and Steve and pointed at the long houses, where we'd guessed the villagers were sleeping. We all nodded to show we understood what he wanted us to do: get the villagers out of them to safety.

Eddie led the way, crawling on hands and knees through the undergrowth, looking for a point near to the long houses from where we could creep into the clearing. I followed Eddie, Benny behind me, and Steve bringing up the rear. The Major and the rest of the unit stayed in hiding, rifles aimed into the clearing in case there was trouble.

We worked our way round the clearing

until we were at the back of the nearest long house. I hoped that there weren't any Communists on guard inside it.

Eddie motioned for me to follow him and for Benny and Steve to lie in wait at the bottom of the bamboo steps up to the house. Eddie and I ran out from the undergrowth, bent double, and made it to the steps without being spotted. We went up them as swiftly as we could, without making a noise.

The entrance to the long house was a doorway with a curtain of palm leaves to keep out insects. We crept in. Inside, about fifty villagers were asleep. The one nearest to us, a man, stirred as we entered. His eyes opened wide in surprise. I hurried to him and placed my free hand gently over his mouth, prompting him to stay quiet. Eddie and I must have looked a terrifying sight. We were covered with muck from the swamp and we were holding rifles.

Remembering how the Major had acted when he had met the locals, I put down my rifle and bowed my head in greeting, putting my hands together as if in prayer. For a second a look of bewilderment crossed the villager's face, then he understood. He knew that the two soldiers strung up on the X-frames were enemies of the Chinese terrorists. Since our uniforms looked like the captured soldiers', it was obvious that we were there to release them and that we meant no harm to the villagers.

The man got up and hurried over to a sleeping woman and shook her awake, whispering urgently as he did so. Soon everyone in the long house was awake. The very small children had been startled at being woken up, but their parents gently hugged and rocked them, reassuring them that everything was all right.

We pointed towards the door, indicating that they were to go outside. The man we had woken first motioned to the others to follow him. One by one, with the smallest children being carried, the villagers climbed nimbly down the bamboo steps to where Benny and Steve were waiting for them. While Benny stayed at the foot of the steps, Steve led the villagers away into the jungle. Soon the long house was empty.

Now Eddie and I headed towards another long house, but a tug at my arm made me stop. I grabbed Eddie to stop him too.

The villager we'd first met had remained behind. He pointed to the long house we were heading to and pulled an expression with his face to make it clear this was not a good idea. I realized that this long house must be filled with terrorists. The villager pointed to another long house and made the same sort of grimaces, so I knew there were more terrorists sleeping there. Then the man pointed to the last long house and indicated that we should go there. It would be full of villagers.

As me, Eddie, Benny and Steve followed him there, I thought how lucky we'd been not to go into either one of the terrorists' long houses. If we had, the whole thing would have burst into a shooting match straight away, and the four of us would probably have been slaughtered.

This time we crouched under the long house while the villager went into it to wake the others. We thought this would be better than us doing it.

As we waited, I heard a baby cry inside

the long house. Obviously it had just been woken up and it was upset at being disturbed. I just hoped its crying wouldn't alarm the terrorists.

I heard scuffling noises above us, then the villagers began to come down the steps.

We came out to join them, Eddie and I keeping guard, while Benny and Steve helped them down the steps and guided them towards the spot where the other villagers had gone. The last villager – an old lady – was just coming down the steps when I heard a noise from one of the terrorists' long houses. Next I saw one of them come to the doorway. When he spotted the line of villagers heading towards the jungle, he began shouting. At the same time, he reached inside and pulled something into view: a machine-gun.

There was no time to wait. One burst from that machine-gun and the villagers would be dead. I raised my rifle, took aim and fired.

The Communist let out a yell and fell backwards.

Steve hurried the villagers out of the

clearing. Benny picked up the old woman at the rear and carried her to safety. From that moment, the whole camp erupted into a mass of gunfire and yelling.

Chapter 16
CHUNG LO

The Communists' HQ was in chaos, like a scene out of hell, lit by the glow from the fires. Greg and Sammy hung from the X-frames as if awaiting sacrifice, with dazzling tracers of bullets flying all around them. The overall sound was deafening.

My rifle shot had brought the terrorist machine-guns into action. In turn, the Major and the rest of the unit came out from cover, firing as they did so.

Benny and I concentrated our fire on the doorway of the long house where I had shot the terrorist. We were trying to keep the terrorists inside it, but they came through the thin bamboo walls, hit the ground, rolled and came up firing.

Communists were also pouring out of the other long house, all armed.

I managed a quick glance at the centre

of the clearing and saw that some of the guys had already reached Greg and Sammy. They were trying to cut them down from the X-frames, but the terrorists' machine-gun posts were causing them problems.

To survive in a chaotic situation like that, you have to keep a clear head and try and watch all directions, as well as keep moving about, ducking and dodging. I did my best to remain cool, which was difficult with bullets flying everywhere. I felt a sudden burning pain in my left upper arm and realized that a burst of bullets had torn away a chunk of flesh. I'd been lucky: an inch nearer and I'd have lost the arm. Another six inches to the right and I'd have been dead, shot through the heart.

There was no time to worry about stopping the bleeding; the nervous adrenalin pumping through my system and the numbness of the shredded nerve endings would keep me on my feet. I turned and let off a round in the direction from which the bullets had come, and saw one of the terrorists crumple to the ground.

The Communists were caught in gunfire

from two sides now: from those of us inside the clearing and from the rest of the guys in the undergrowth round it. One problem was that, if we weren't careful, we could end up shooting our own men.

I saw Eddie go down as a burst of gunfire hit him. I retaliated with a bullet at the terrorist who'd shot him. The whole clearing was just a wall of sound – gunfire and screams.

Then, above all the noise, I heard very loud shouting in what sounded like Chinese: the same phrase repeated over and over again. The gunfire subsided.

I also stopped firing, but remained ready for action.

The Major was in the centre of the clearing, standing over the body of a Communist who lay face down on the ground. The Communist was still alive, but the Major had one foot on the back of his neck, pinning him down, while holding his gun to the back of the man's head.

The Major shouted in Chinese at the terrorist. The man turned his head and muttered a reply. The Major shouted at him again. The Communist repeated what he'd said, only louder this time. The other terrorists looked at one another, as if wondering what to do. In the silence, there was a metallic click as the Major pulled back the trigger of his gun, the barrel pressed against the Communist's head. Now the man shouted much louder, a note of panic in his voice.

In response, the other terrorists threw down their weapons.

The Major called out an order in Chinese and the terrorists spread-eagled themselves on the ground.

'Collect up their weapons,' said the Major.

While the others did this, I hurried over to Eddie. He was alive, but bleeding badly. He'd taken a burst across his chest and right shoulder. It looked bad. I was tearing off his shirt to get to the wounds, when I felt a tap on my shoulder.

I looked round to see that it was one of the villagers. Then I became aware that all the villagers had come back from the safety of the jungle.

The villager pointed at Eddie and then at the women standing nearby. Other villagers were going around, checking on our soldiers who were lying on the ground. I realized that the villager was telling me that the women would take care of Eddie.

One of the women came up to me. She was only about half my height. She reached out and gently touched my bleeding left arm and motioned to me to sit down on the ground.

The Major had left the Communist on the ground with two of our guys, who were tying him up. He came over to Eddie, a look of concern on his face. He said something to the village man in his language, and the man answered him. The Major watched as the women started to clean Eddie's wounds with leaves. Then the Major came over to me. The woman who was attending to me was also using leaves on my wound to gently wipe off the blood.

'Let them do whatever they want,' the Major said. 'They know which plants are antiseptic. They'll take care of you.'

'What about Eddie?' I asked. 'He's been shot in the chest.'

The Major frowned.

'I don't know,' he said. 'They'll do their best. If they can stabilize him, we'll get a chopper to winch him out quickly.' He gestured around to the other wounded soldiers. 'Same with the rest of the boys who need urgent treatment.'

I pointed at the man who the Major had taken prisoner.

'I assume that's Chung Lo?' I said.

'Yes,' said the Major. 'He's changed since that last photo, but there was something about him that was familiar. Something about the look in his eyes.'

He stared at me and, then, for the first time since I'd met him, I thought I saw a slight smile on his face.

'You did well, Taggart,' he said. 'So, now it's up to you. Looks like the war here in Malaya is over, with Chung Lo finally brought to book. You can return to prison back in England or you can stay with the SAS. I'll give you time to think it over.'

I grinned.

'No time needed, Major,' I said. 'I'm staying with the SAS.'

As the Major remarked, with the capture of Chung Lo and his men, the war in Malaya was all but over.

Out of the hundred of us who'd gone into the Telok Anson swamp, seventeen men died: the ten men of Unit Two, plus Terry Swift and the six men who were killed in that final battle in the terrorists' HQ in the heart of the jungle.

Amazingly, Eddie Kershaw recovered and a year later he was back in action with the SAS. Chester Harris also pulled through, but he returned home to England and was invalided out of the army.

Benny also decided he'd stay with the SAS. He and I became part of the same four-man team within the squadron. But the adventures we had after Malaya . . . well, that's for another time.

HISTORICAL NOTE

Although this book is fiction, it is based on real events.

In 1948 the Chinese in Malaya who supported Communist China began a guerrilla war against the British, Malaya's rulers. By March 1950 the Communist guerrillas had killed hundreds of people, civilian and military. In 1952 the CTs (as these Chinese terrorists were known) assassinated the British Governor of Malaya, Sir Henry Gurney, in an ambush. As a result the re-formed SAS was sent in to knock out the CTs. Between 1952 and 1957 the SAS began to take shape as it learned from its jungle experiences. By 1958 it had effectively become the SAS that we know today.

The bulk of the fighting in Malaya was carried out by the regular army. At the height of the 'Malayan Emergency', as it was known, 22 battalions of British and Commonwealth infantry were used, as well as 180,000 police and 250,000 Home Guards. In the twelve years the campaign lasted, 6,400 CTs were killed and a further 3,000 were captured or surrendered. Most of these were the result of actions by the Brigade of Gurkhas, the Suffolk Regiment, the Scots Guards and the Commando Brigade.

However, it was during the Emergency that the re-formed SAS really perfected its skill of surviving and beating an enemy in the jungle.

In February 1958, 37 men of SAS D Squadron, under the command of Harry Thompson, parachuted into the Telok Anson swamp. Their mission was to capture (or kill) two groups of CTs hiding there. These CTs were led by Ah Hoi.

Because the men were parachuting into jungle, some were injured when they landed among the trees.

After landing, there was a ten-day trek along river banks and through swamps which varied in depth from shin-high to neck-high. The soldiers were prey to leeches, which could drink half a pint of their blood before being detected.

An SAS troop commanded by Peter de la Billière hunted Ah Hoi's terrorists following a route through the swamps along the Tengi river. They realized that Ah Hoi and his men knew they were being pursued and were managing to keep one step ahead of them.

At the same time, a separate SAS troop under Sergeant Sandilands travelled through the swamp by night. They were hoping to catch Ah Hoi's men in a pincer movement with de la Billière's troop.

After twenty days in the swamp, all the men were suffering from various infections. De la Billière's legs, ripped by thorns, had become infected, and they were now a mass of ulcers.

Finally, after twenty-two days, a woman came out of the jungle and identified herself to the security forces at a checkpoint as Ah Niet, Ah Hoi's messenger. Ah Hoi wished to do a deal: he demanded his freedom, a payment of £3,500 to each of his followers and an amnesty for the CTs already in prison. The reply was: no deal. Ah Hoi had a choice of surrendering within twenty-four hours or the RAF would bomb his position in the jungle and kill him and his guerrillas.

As a result, Ah Hoi came out of the jungle with his men and surrendered. He was sent into exile in China.

The Malayan Emergency came to an end in 1960.

SAS JUNGLE TRAINING

The jungle part of the selection process for the SAS takes place at the Jungle Training School in Brunei. Brunei is in South-east Asia on the island of Borneo, between the Malaysian states of Sarawak and Sabah. The training course lasts six weeks.

The jungle is a hostile environment, with danger present in both the flora (the plants) and the fauna (the wildlife).

In between the bamboo trees, which grow to enormous heights, will be found long spiky vines that can trap people. Some of the plants have leaves with 'fish-hook' thorns at the end, which catch on to skin. If you are caught by any of these, do not struggle and try to pull away because this will only make the situation worse. The answer is to remove the thorns that cling to your skin as gently as you can.

Because of this kind of dangerous undergrowth, it is often best to travel through jungle using the streams, rivers and swamps. However, this can lead to your body being covered in leeches, which live in the water. It used to be said that if you picked off a leech that was feeding on you, its head would be left in your skin and cause infection. However, recent studies have suggested that leeches can be picked off safely. If they prove difficult to remove, there are two ways to get them off: put salt on them or burn them off with a smouldering piece of wood.

The only way to travel safely through jungle is slowly.

SLEEPING AND SHELTER

When finding a place to sleep in the jungle, it is always best to make a raised platform so that your bed is off the ground. This is because most of the reptiles, such as snakes, and insects which can harm you, live on the ground.

Building such a platform is fairly easy in the jungle because you are surrounded by bamboo and strong vines to tie the lengths of bamboo together. When the platform has been made, lay out palm leaves on top of it to make a basic 'mattress'. Alternatively, you can sleep in a hammock suspended from a frame made of bamboo.

If you are going to be staying in one place for long, build a shelter round your raised platform. Again, use bamboo and the large leaves from palm trees for a roof and walls. A living space in the jungle made in this way is called a *basha*.

If you have made a fire for cooking, spread its ash round where the bamboo stakes of your *basha* touch the ground, because this will help to keep insects away.

CROSSING A RIVER IN THE JUNGLE

Find a part of the river where the current is slowest. This is usually where it is widest. (At a narrow point in a river the water is 'squeezed', increasing its force. Water also tends to flow faster where there is a bend in the river.)

The safest way for a troop to cross a river is for the lead soldier to take the end of a rope with him. He should always cross the river walking against the current. Before he sets off, another rope will be attached to him, which is held by two men on the bank. So, if the man crossing should slip and be washed downriver, he can be pulled safely back to the bank.

When the lead soldier reaches the other side, he secures the end of the rope he was carrying, perhaps round a nearby tree. The troop can then clip their karabiners to the rope and make their way safely across. (A karabiner is a snap ring used for latching on to a rope.) The last man across unties the end of the rope before wading across, while the other men keep hold of the rope, ready to pull him to safety if necessary.

HEALTH HAZARDS IN THE JUNGLE

DISEASES FROM INSECTS

MALARIA

CAUSE: Transmitted through the saliva of the female mosquito.
SYMPTOMS: Fever. Patient feels very cold and shivers violently, although sweating. Patient feels weak and exhausted. Sometimes headaches and vomiting also occur.
TREATMENT: Anti-malaria tablets.

DENGUE

CAUSE: Caught from mosquitoes.
SYMPTOMS: Fever, headache, skin rash, very painful joints and muscles.
TREATMENT: No known treatment.

TYPHUS

CAUSE: Caught from tiny insects such as ticks, mites and fleas.
SYMPTOMS: Headache, constipation, coughing and back pain, followed by fever. Skin rash of small red spots.
TREATMENT: Antibiotics.

YELLOW FEVER

CAUSE: Transmitted through the saliva of the female mosquito.
SYMPTOMS: Nosebleed, headache, nausea, fever. Liver damage may lead to kidney failure and jaundice.
TREATMENT: No effective drug treatment; can be prevented by an injection beforehand.

DISEASES FROM WATER

HOOKWORM

CAUSE: Hookworms get inside the body after a person has drunk water infected with them. They can also penetrate the body through the skin. The worms live in the intestines and can cause pneumonia.
TREATMENT: Drinking the liquid from boiled-up bracken.

BILHARZIA

CAUSE: Microscopic worms entering the body after drinking water containing them, or sometimes through broken skin. They cause diseases of the bowel or bladder.
SYMPTOMS: Irritation of urinary tract.
TREATMENT: Prescribed drugs.

AMOEBIC DYSENTERY

CAUSE: Dirty water or food.
SYMPTOMS: Fatigue. High temperature. Diarrhoea which smells foul and contains blood and a red jelly-like mucus.

TREATMENT: A powerful drug called Metroni-dazole.

DANGEROUS JUNGLE CREATURES

ELECTRIC EELS

About 2 metres long and 20 cm thick, they are found in shallow water in rivers in South America. Can give a shock of 500 volts.

PIRANHA FISH

Found in rivers in South America, they have large jaws with razor-sharp, interlocking teeth.

CROCODILES AND ALLIGATORS

These include:
● the saltwater crocodile (man-eating crocodile found in Malaysia, India, Australia)
● the black cayman (found in South America)
● the mugger (a marsh crocodile found in India)
● the American alligator (found in south-eastern USA)
● the African crocodile, which lives in both salt and fresh water.

SNAKES

These include:
● the Malay pit viper, which is very poisonous. It can be fawn-coloured, or red or grey, marked with geometric patterns.

The belly is yellow or a spotted greenish-brown. About 60—80 cm long, it is found in South-east Asia.

Russell's viper. A very poisonous snake, brownish with three rows of spots of white-bordered black rings with a reddish-brown centre. About 1.25 metres long, it is found in the region from Taiwan west to Pakistan.

the cottonmouth. A very dangerous snake with a browny-green body with a yellowish belly. About 60—130 cm long, it is found in or by fresh water in the southern USA.

POISONOUS PLANTS FOUND IN THE JUNGLE

- **PANGI**: found mainly in Malaysia. All parts of the plant are deadly poisonous, especially the fruit, which contains prussic acid.

  STRYCHNINE: mainly found in India. The seeds are deadly poisonous.

  CASTOR-OIL PLANT: the seeds act as a violent purgative and are sometimes fatal.

  DUCHESNIA: found in Asia and North America. Deadly.

  PHYSIC NUT: the seeds taste sweet but are a violent purgative.

  NETTLE TREE: the sting is similar to common nettle, only much worse. The seeds are poisonous.

  WHITE MANGROVE: found in swamps. It causes blisters and blindness.